Jeet's agent, Maggie, and her husband, Ed, seemed to think that Jeet's assumption about Flora and the Mia-suited woman was a hundred percent correct.

"They were definitely working together," Maggie offered, looking at me. "The woman who knocked you down and the one who picked you up."

"Oh, for God's sake," I said. "Maybe you and Ed are in on it, too. Maybe you're supposed to lure us away from our room. Because then they can have a clear shot at stealing, I don't know, our travel alarm clock. And my nightgown. And, God, let me think. What other precious things do we have up there?"

They both looked puzzled. They looked at each other and then at Jeet. Jeet, of course, knew that I was exaggerating for comic effect, but these two didn't seem to have a clue. "Thank God," I continued, "that I left the tiara at home."

GROOMED FOR DEATH

Carolyn Banks

FAWCETT GOLD MEDAL • NEW YORK

A Fawcett Gold Medal Book
Published by Ballantine Books
Copyright © 1995 by Carolyn Banks

Library of Congress Catalog Card Number: 94-94650

ISBN 0-449-14913-7

Printed in Canada

First Edition: February 1995

10 9 8 7 6 5 4

For T. E. D. Klein
il miglior fabbro.

Author's Note

I want to thank Paul Novograd, who owns Claremont Riding Academy, for letting me set this bit of hanky-panky on the premises. For the record, I'd like to state that none of the dastardly activities that take place in this mystery have *ever* gone on at Claremont, or, for that matter, any other riding stable I have visited. I'd also like to thank Sydney Wood, Susan Rudolph, and members of the Claremont staff, for answering all of my questions and providing me with a guided tour of the more-than-century-old building. Laura Rose, of the National Sporting Library in Middleburg, Virginia, helped me with the research, as did Ted Klein and Sheronda Copeland, and I was given terrific comments that aided in the structuring and revision of this manuscript by Jeff Hartman, William Browning Spencer, Elisa Wares, Janis Rizzo and Vicky Bijur. I'd also like to thank Susan Gueneau for the wonderful fetlock anecdote that I attributed to Flora. I'm grateful, too, to Mouse—the only character in the book who exists in real life. His size and demeanor inspired me to include him.

CHAPTER 1

"What I'm looking forward to," my husband said, "is a week without horses."

"Shhh," I told him. It was seven-something in the morning, and daylight was beginning to dapple our bedroom. "They'll hear you." I didn't mean that their feelings would be hurt, of course. I meant, literally, that they'd hear our voices and know that we were up.

Or, to put it more exactly, that *I* was up. And being *up*, I should be out there toting grain and hay, refreshing their water, and otherwise ministering to them, right?

Horses can be tyrants.

Especially my horses. Plum, my aged mare, had been relatively sedate about making her morning demands known. She'd, at most, rattle the rubber pail that hung along the fence line, a sound you could more or less sleep through.

Then she acquired a pasture mate, Spier, who taught her to be more assertive. Now Plum joined him in beating her hooves on the metal water trough the very minute a sign of life issued from the house (and of course, just before daybreak, they were always positioned to stare at the house).

1

Think of the drum break in Edgar Winter's "Franken-stein."

Think of the drum break as if played by a student drummer.

A pair of student drummers, student drummers wielding ball peen hammers.

So of course I knew what Jeet was talking about when he fantasized a horseless week in New York City. A week of maybe snuggling for a minute or two before duty forced me to bound out of bed.

And sound carries in this part of Texas. My best friend, Lola, who lives with her boyfriend, Cody, on the farm next door, hinted around about it, and none too subtly.

"They make rubber troughs," she said.

"I've priced them," I told her. "Plus it seems criminal to throw a perfectly good metal one away."

"So have a yard sale," she suggested.

"Who would come to this yard?" Because Jeet and I live in really rural Texas. I mean, not prime yard-sale territory. And since everyone else I knew lived similarly, a yard sale did not seem in the cards.

"You could advertise it in the newsletter." She meant our dressage-club newsletter.

"Hmmm," I said. This meant I wouldn't and Lola knew it.

But I am changing the subject here. The subject is Jeet and his upcoming New York jaunt, via which he was to become—we hoped—a published author, not just of restaurant critiques, which he regularly does for the *Austin Daily Progress*, but of a book, a memoir about the food he had eaten growing up.

Jeet's proposal had attracted the attention of a New York agent Jeet had met at one of the many food deals he gets invited to. This was a dim sum, I think, held in Houston. What the agent had been doing there, I hadn't the vaguest, but she had persuaded Jeet to put a memory or two down on paper, along with a table of contents, and the next thing I knew, we were being invited to meet with an actual New York publisher who wanted to see how marketable Jeet was.

"God, Robin," Jeet said now, his voice, alas, rising into a range audible to hungry equines who began to beat their morning tattoo, "I could end up with a cooking show on television or something. The galloping gourmet."

"Galloping, right," I scoffed, sliding a pair of jeans on over my bare bottom and pulling boots on over sockless feet. Horses, to my husband, were merely an evil necessary to cohabitation with me, so *galloping* did not seem an appellation that might be considered apt.

"I'm not kidding," Jeet said, handing me a T-shirt that looked as though it had been under his pillow for weeks. It may have been, too. Housekeeping is not one of my strengths.

I yanked it on. Outside, what had begun as a relatively tentative *bam-bam-bam* had risen to a fever pitch. I could picture Spier in a former life as a human, squatting over a pair of stretched zebra-skin drums that were the tribal equivalent of CNN.

The phone rang just as I raised the window and screamed out like some tenement dweller, "I'm coming already!"

"It's Lola," Jeet was saying as I hurled myself into the stairwell. "She wants to kill you."

But minutes later contentment descended on our little Primrose Farm.

By which I mean that the minute I appeared in the flesh, the metallic pounding stopped. Plum gave a grateful nicker. Then both horses went off to pee while I measured out their grain.

Don't ask. I don't have a clue. This is just what they do, morning after morning after morning. You can hear them peeing, as if they've stored it up for just this moment, and on chilly mornings, steam rises from the pool of urine that foams at their feet.

For some reason, I find this wonderful and reassuring, although I admit that until this very moment, I have never said this out loud to anyone.

God, I *need* a week in New York City, a week in a place where the only horses are ridden by police into unruly mobs or else pull hansom cabs. Or maybe appear on billboards in ads for sophisticated clothing: Mia, say, or Ralph Lauren.

Which reminds me.

New York City is still a major deal to Texans. I'm not kidding. A lot of people I know have never been to New York. So they feel compelled to express their fears and pass on general observations.

Such as (this was Suzie Ballinger, who was present at my last riding lesson): "New York! Oh, no! You'll be ritually murdered."

"Naw," I told Suzie, "that's California. New York is

where they knock you down in the street and take your jewelry."

This conversation took place while I was riding Plum in my coach, Wanda's, huge indoor arena. I should have realized something was afoot because of the way Wanda was staring at me when I said this. A sort of other-worldly stare, into what I think is called the middle distance.

"Yes," Wanda said, in her wavy heebie-jeebie voice, a voice she reserves for her psychic moments. "Yes." Very Californian.

Wanda *comes* from California. She's into all this mind-body and imagery stuff and she even hangs crystals in her horses' stalls. She talks about reincarnation all the time, but that does make a certain amount of sense. As she puts it, who can learn to ride dressage in a single lifetime?

"We were working on haunches-in," I said, verbally nudging her in the direction of my lesson, which, after all, was costing me thirty-five bucks an hour.

Wanda looked up at the skylights of the indoor, sucked her breath in audibly, threw her hands in front of her face, and hunched over, as though the roof were about to fall in on her.

"Oh, no," I said, forgetting, momentarily, all about riding. "Wanda, tell me."

She composed herself. "It's nothing," she said. "Let's proceed with the work at hand."

I was so eager to find out what Wanda had seen that I managed to get Plum to do what is—for me—a pretty sophisticated movement, haunches-in, the horse's body bent around my leg, her haunches off the track, but her front legs still on the track as if she were proceeding normally. If you don't get it, don't worry, it takes a while to lock this into your mind.

Eventually I was able to draw Wanda back to what she had seen and feared. In the cryptic fashion that is her wont, she said, "Something will fall from the sky. It will affect you greatly. From the sky."

An optimist would think of raining dollar bills. I guess I'm not one. Because, of course, during the intervening week I thought about the flight to New York. The flight to New York plummeting to the tundra somewhere between Texas and Newark Airport.

I don't like to fly. In fact, the stewardess just about has to rock me.

It's probably a control thing. Dressage riders are notoriously into control. But whatever it is, up there in the great beyond, I'm scared.

I mean, I wouldn't be scared if the pilot would announce that he's turning left or right, but of course, pilots don't. They just do it, and I kind of reflexively gasp. This is a singular behavioral advance, by the way; I used to shriek. But anyway, when the plane just turns that way, without warning, I gasp and then everyone stares at me.

Not that I'm not used to everyone staring at me.

It's a particular kind of stare, too. The kind that people like to share with others.

But I'm getting ahead of myself. I was telling you about the sort of remark an announcement that you're going to New York pulls out of Texans.

One such is, "What are you going to wear?"

In my case, despite the dearth of clothing, fashionable and otherwise, in my closet, I have the perfect answer:

"These," I say, indicating the formfitting cotton-cum-Lycra breeches that I've taken to wearing almost always. They are actually the most comfortable thing I own. Plus they look like leggings, which people still seem to be wearing.

And they're black and therefore an essential part of what I think of as the standard fat girl's outfit. (I have been wearing the standard fat girl's outfit for years, though technically speaking, I'm a yo-yo, up and down, depending on the strength of my willpower.) But anyway, to get back to the reported conversation at hand, after gesturing at my breeches, I say, "And lots of tops." Dressy tops and comfy tees. Add a pair of flats and voilà! New York, here I come.

I got home just after Jeet. He was still in the clothes that he had worn to work: khakis and a white dress shirt. He looked incredibly preppy, but sexy nonetheless.

He stood on the porch as I lumbered up the driveway in Mother—my truck—my Warmblood-sized trailer with Plum inside in tow. That is, my 7½ ft. tall, 18 ft. long trailer, ready to receive a gargantuan horse, with a relatively normal-sized animal inside it.

He watched me wheel it around and park it, a look of admiration on his face. This is because Jeet is daunted by the size of the rig and has never attempted to drive it. He therefore thinks it immensely difficult, and loves me all the more for mastery of the task.

I let him go on thinking it, although anyone who's

ever pulled a horse trailer knows that it's a relatively simple procedure, particularly if the horse inside is still. My horses tend to go into a state of somnambulance once loaded. It's the loading that's tough.

Of course, there's backing the rig. Now that's worthy of all of Jeet's near awe. Particularly if you're among the uncoordinated, and you don't respond well to directions like, "Turn the wheel in the direction opposite to the one you want to go."

Right.

Who prescribed this, the Delphic oracle?

If you're among the uncoordinated, don't even try to think this through. Instead, put your hand at the bottom of the steering wheel and turn the way you'd turn ordinarily. Great, huh? A woman named Mary Beth Ruspino taught me this invaluable tip.

But back to the story.

So there's Jeet, all smiles, standing at my rolled-down window. "Good lesson?" he asks.

"Yes, but"—I take time out for a little kiss—"Wanda had a psychic moment and . . ."

Jeet gets that look.

"No, really," I continue. "She saw something falling out of the sky—"

"And you think it's the plane," he interrupted.

"Well . . ." I slid out and shut the truck door. He followed me around to the back of the trailer, even though I knew he wasn't dying to hear about Wanda's vision.

Sure enough, "Tell me about your lesson," he urged.

Jeet sure knows how to change a subject. I warmed to it, telling him how good Wanda thought my seat was getting, even as I let Plum back out onto the gravel.

Jeet held her lead shank while I undid her tail wrap and the wraps I'd put on her legs. We walked her out to the pasture together and watched as she whinnied for Spier.

From somewhere deep in the hollow, he answered her. She galloped off to be with him.

"The gate must be closed down there," I said. Otherwise, Spier would have followed the trailer down the driveway, herd instinct being what it is.

"I'd go with you," Jeet said, "but I've got something in the oven."

What a man.

If Wanda had foreseen what *he* would go through on our trip, I'd have canceled it. But right before the trip, there were no omens, no hints, no clues. No turkey vultures sitting on the telephone wires watching.

"Oooh," I said when I got back into the house. "I have to show you how the woman at the feed store told me to carry my purse." This was a cautionary tip by someone who watched *NYPD Blue* all the time.

I demonstrated, hunching over as if trying out for the part of the bell ringer in some gothic play. "I would rather lose my purse," I told Jeet, "I swear."

"I dunno," my husband said. "I think it's kind of cute. We could change your name to Igor and you could hang out in some cobwebbed place."

"The subway," I offered.

"No. Absolutely not the subway," Jeet said. "That's where everybody at the paper says you shouldn't go. Right after Central Park." Then he all of a sudden got serious. "I mean it," he said. "No subway. Take cabs. Or better still, don't leave the hotel room at all."

"Now, *that* sounds like fun." I could take up needlepoint or crossword puzzles or something.

"No, I mean it," he said, wagging his finger, which he only does when he is very serious. "New York can be a dangerous place and—"

"Relax," I told him, momentarily forgetting even Wanda, "nothing bad will happen."

CHAPTER 2

Now that we were actually *in* New York, Jeet was nervous again. I was surprised that he wasn't making sure that I'd be okay by dragging me along to the meeting with his agent and soon-to-be publisher, but I guess it would have looked unprofessional. And Jeet had tried very hard to look professional, even opting for one of those tweed jackets with suede elbow patches.

"What do you think?" He'd stood in front of the mirror at Second Looks, which was a used men's-clothing store in Austin.

"Even though you are my husband," I purred, "if we weren't in public, I would toss you to the carpet and—"

The salesman cleared his throat and Jeet, I swear, flushed. But he bought the jacket, which was made of melton wool and had a chichi London label. Perfect for spring in NYC.

He was wearing it now in our moderately priced hotel room.

"But do I *look* like a writer?" he was asking.

"What difference does it make?" I threw back. "You *are* a writer." He'd brought a portfolio of clips to prove

11

it, stuff he'd done for the newspaper on all kinds of cuisine.

This morning, in the artificially darkened hotel room, we'd managed to snuggle for a long, long time, both of us indulging in fantasies of what it would be like when Jeet wrote books instead of newspaper articles and made tons of money and we didn't have to scrape along anymore.

Jeet was talking hot tubs and Cancún vacations when I guess I spoiled the mood.

"Mmmm," I said. "We could get a tractor." And before I could describe the accessories I wanted—a chain harrow, maybe, and a front-end loader for sure, Jeet was upright, searching for his shoes.

That's the way it goes when one person is a horse person and the other one isn't. But I forgave Jeet his lack of interest and loved him all the same. After all, every woman I knew, just about, was in the same She Rides, He Doesn't boat.

"Maybe I look too preppy," Jeet was saying now, still posing in front of the mirror. It was very unlike him. "Maybe they're expecting me to be, I don't know, Texan or something."

I imagined my husband in boots and a ten-gallon hat and laughed. He was tall and lanky enough, for sure, but he just wasn't, I don't know, countrified.

"You don't think I could pull it off?" he asked.

"You could pull it off until you started talking about béchamel sauce or something. Sauce velouté."

"That's not bad," Jeet said now, commenting, I knew, on my pronunciation. He had schooled me rigorously in such matters, though basically I couldn't have cared less. It was Jeet who had majored in home economics, not me.

The first time I'd had him over to dinner—I mean back a hundred years ago when we started dating—I'd made Kraft macaroni and cheese, which I'd dressed up by adding a tablespoon of desiccated parsley. I think that's when he decided he had to rescue me by making me his wife.

"You'd better get going," I said, gesturing at the travel clock we'd brought with us.

"Remember—" he began.

"I know, I know," I interrupted in order to kiss him good-bye. "I won't use public toilets. I won't talk to strangers. I will look both ways before I cross the street. And I'll—"

"You can make fun if you like, Robin," Jeet said, "but I can't help worrying. You're too trusting for a city like New York."

I made a sour face, but he kissed me again anyway, and then he was on his way. He knew he'd be getting a scrumptious lunch on somebody's expense account, so we weren't doing breakfast, which was fine with me.

The minute he was gone I flung the window open and looked down into the street. The barrage of noise— honking horns and jackhammers and distant sirens and assorted hollering—was instantaneous and exciting. The writer O. Henry—who was big in Austin because he'd lived there—had likened New York City to Baghdad. Even though I'd never been to Baghdad, I sensed that he was right.

The life I ordinarily lead on our little four-acre

spread, Primrose Farm, is essentially boring, though in a reassuring sort of way. What I mean by this is that, except for the aforementioned banging on the water trough that the horses indulge in at mealtime, crickets and coyotes and the occasional whinny is about all you hear.

Even in Austin, which is, like, twenty-some miles away from our place, you don't hear what I was hearing in New York. Because New York has a kind of, I don't know, a welled-up teemingness, a tallness, that Austin doesn't really have. (Thank your stars that Jeet is the writer and not me! Teemingness! God!)

I could hardly wait to get outside.

And I wasn't disappointed, either. Because, added to the sounds that were loud and rude and everywhere were the smells emanating from the stands of the various food vendors. There were fruit smells and pretzel smells and eggroll smells, all warring with one another.

Not that you caught any more than the briefest whiff, because you were kind of swept along in the New York pace.

I'm not kidding. Everyone seemed in a hurry, and if you dawdled there on the pavement, you probably would have been trampled by not just one, but maybe several people. So I walked along feeling as if I were speedwalking.

It was wonderful, like being in that old Audrey Hepburn movie *Breakfast at Tiffany's*. I could imagine being—I don't know—a budding actress or a dancer and coming to New York to seek my fortune, make my way.

Even the thought of people bursting into song the

way they do in musicals didn't seem weird. This was the city of infinite possibility.

I even liked the panhandlers.

We have panhandlers in Austin, of course, but the panhandlers in New York were more plentiful. And more aggressive, too. They didn't just hold up signs about their plight. They actually spoke. Of course, in Austin, you're not walking much, you're sort of driving everywhere, so of course, a panhandler would have to be content with holding up a sign. But in New York, where you're on the street . . .

Anyway, the panhandlers in New York were also pretty funny. I gave money to a guy collecting for the United Negro Pizza Fund, for instance, and to yet another who said he was amassing a down payment for a condominium.

I don't know, New York just didn't seem very dangerous to me. On the side streets, though, I'd see evidence that it was on some of the cars that were parked at the curb. They'd have signs in the windows saying things like STEREO ALREADY STOLEN and EVERYTHING OF VALUE ALREADY GONE. Without these signs, though, I'd have concluded that life here was a sort of idyll.

I'd see old people, for instance, being shepherded around by young folks obviously hired to do just that. And they were doing it lovingly, not perfunctorily—you know, some tough-looking kid with a ring in his nose pushing along an old black lady in a wheelchair, that kind of thing. And the kid and the old lady would be keeping up a steady line of patter, really talking.

And there were flowers. Flowers in window boxes, flowers in clay pots, violas and dianthus and sweet peas—the kind of flowers that could withstand a spring-time frost.

Flowers. Humor. Communion between young and old. That had to mean that New York was a nice place, right?

At first I had no destination, but eventually, a likely one dawned on me: Miller's. I would go to Miller's, the famed riding store that sent catalogs out to hundreds of thousands of horse people all over the country, including me. Several times a year Miller's gets our collective covet mechanisms churning, and we lust after such things as fuchsia bell boots for our horses, fuchsia schooling sweats for ourselves. In Texas, where a trip to New York is a major deal, there are even Miller's rumors. That there's a bargain basement in the NYC store, for instance.

Bargain basement. That's a laugh. If there were one, it would be worth a trek to the East Coast, believe me, because everything that has to do with horses, from a simple plastic mane-and-tail comb on up, costs major bucks.

But now I was here, I reasoned, I could go to Miller's and find out for myself. I practically salivated thinking about it, and meanwhile patted the wadded-up fifty dollars that Jeet had given me as spending money for our four-day jaunt. He'd given me a credit card, too, but that was for emergencies.

I tried asking the way, but the people who were willing to stop didn't seem to know what Miller's was. They tried, though. It sort of went like this:

"Miller's. It's a bar, right?" This was a guy buying a paper at a corner newsstand.

"No, it's a store. It's a riding store."

"A writing store? Like you need a tablet, or what?"

After a few conversations of this sort, I decided I would look the address up in a phone book.

New York City has dozens of outdoor phones. None of them, however, comes with a book. Nor—considering the absence of shelving of any sort—did a book ever appear to be part of the scheme. So I'd try information, usually depositing, and losing, a quarter in the process.

Not that the information operator didn't come on. It's just that I was rarely able to hear her, what with the cacophony of the streets. I'd shout. She'd shout. And we'd usually end up with:

"Sweetie, there are a dozen Millers in the directory here."

"But this is a store," I'd protest. "This is a riding store."

"What is it you want to buy? A tablet?"

No, info ops can't look in the Yellow Pages. And no, they never stay on the line long enough to even let you ask for an address, although I understand that these days they're actually allowed to give you one if you can hold their attention for the length of time that it would take to ask.

And this isn't easy. I mean, these days you aren't even sure you have the phone company, because they don't say "information" or "directory assistance" anymore, they say, "This is Dolores," or, "This is Steve," and you have to ask, "With the phone company?"

But the real pisser is that the quarter you've deposited doesn't come back out the way it's supposed to.

I mentioned this loudly as I beat on the box with the heel of my hand, and a man in the street chastised me.

"What, you want miracles?" he asked. "Just be glad you have a phone to use that's working, girlie. Count your blessings, that's what I say."

I waited until he was out of my hearing range and then I called the operator. "Listen," I said, "I have been losing quarters right and left. I have lost about a dollar fifty so far and I demand that the phone company mail me a refund." So there.

"Well, why did you keep putting quarters in?" the operator twanged.

"Because I had to make a call, that's why. I had to make a call."

"Give me the number," she said, "and I'll put it through for you."

"I don't know the number. I was calling information."

"You were calling information?"

"Information."

She sighed. She weighed, I suppose, my seeming sincerity against her well-honed New York instincts. "Give me your address," she said. "But listen, sweetie, don't use those street phones, okay? I mean, if you're sure you're gonna get an answer, fine, but otherwise, forget about your quarters. You're just throwing quarters away, you know what I mean?"

"What *do* you mean?" I asked. Were New York phones set up to eat the customers' change or what?

"I mean there's street kids who rig those phones. They stuff them with plastic trash bags, okay? And then they go back with a coat hanger and pull the trash bags out and there's all this money that people lost that comes out, too, see what I'm saying?"

"You're kidding," I said.

"No. That's what they do."

"Wow."

"So don't use those street phones, all right?"

"All right," I assured her. "And thanks for telling me."

I can't explain it, but I liked knowing that. I like inside information. And information about New York City seemed especially inside.

I smiled and kept on walking and soon found I had wandered way up Broadway. Just being on Broadway—a street I'd heard so much about—was, in and of itself, pretty exciting. I looked around for theaters and stars, but didn't see a one. Evidently I wasn't on the right part of Broadway for that.

I had been walking for more than an hour, and by this time I was at eighty-something, and the streets were teeming with life and music and people of every color and description. Stores selling everything—towels, fruit, electronic stuff—were open to the street.

The buildings were fairly low here, but there was something distinctly un-Texan about the scene. I watched the flow of traffic and tried to figure out what distinguished this place from, say, Sixth Street in Austin.

Ah! Not a single pickup truck. That was it. I walked on, comforted by the fact that I'd managed to solve the little mystery I'd posed for myself.

Still, I hadn't a clue about how to get to the fabled

riding-goods store, or even if I was going in the right direction.

Maybe, I thought, I should change my goal. Head for the New York Public Library or one of the museums I'd heard about or something.

Of course, I didn't have an address for any of those, either, but people on the street would be more likely to know about those than about Miller's, right?

Then it hit me. A New York City cabdriver would know. All I had to do was flag down a cab and I could go anywhere I wanted—Miller's, the Guggenheim, the Metropolitan Opera, the Empire State Building, you name it.

There certainly were taxis everywhere, dozens of them. The trouble was, I wasn't able to get even one to stop. I mean, there I was out on the curb, waving my arms and hollering "Taxi," just like in the movies, but they just kept right on driving by. Some, I saw as they grew near, already had a passenger or two on board. Others must have been on their way to pick passengers up. Maybe, I thought, you had to learn how to put your fingers in your mouth and whistle in order to get one.

Finally rush hour seemed to have died down, because the flow of traffic—foot and otherwise—all but ceased. And sure enough, I was able to wave and have a cab actually cruise on over to the curb as if to pick me up.

I say "as if" because it never actually happened. Oh, the cab did stop, all right, but just as I reached for the door handle, I was mugged.

Well, maybe not mugged, because I'm not sure what mugging actually entails. I mean, no one took any of my money. Still, the woman in question—a well-dressed, okay-looking woman, too—actually grabbed my arms and pulled me backward and then tripped me or something, causing me to fall in a heap right there on the street.

I landed on my backside, my purse rolling into the gutter and spilling its contents all over the pavement. Then, as I watched in openmouthed amazement, the woman wrenched the cab door open, got inside, and was driven away.

"Hey!" I heard myself yelling. "Hey!"

I couldn't get over the fact that this was not some bag lady, but a woman in a suit, a woman with a matching purse and shoes.

The next thing I knew, I was being helped to my feet by a frizzy-haired Hispanic girl who was wearing the biggest earrings I have ever seen.

"The nerve of some people," she said, looking off in the direction of the taxi. Then to me: "You hurt?"

"No," I said, bending to pick up the array of belongings at my feet.

The girl bent down to help me. "Oooh," she said, picking up a book I'd brought with me on the off chance I had to wait in line or something. It was a title I'd been trying, without any success, to get to back home: *The Athletic Development of the Dressage Horse: Manège Patterns* by Charles deKunffy. Not exactly the sort of book you curl up with. But the girl seemed riveted by it. "You ride?" she asked me, handing it back.

"Yeah," I said. But I wasn't surprised by her query.

After all, the book did have a picture of a horse doing half pass on the cover.

"My name's Flora, by the way," she said, sticking out a small brown hand with bright purple fingernails. "I'm kind of a horse nut myself. You a tourist, or what?"

"I'm sort of a tourist," I said. "Except that I haven't been anywhere yet."

Flora laughed. "Where is it you want to go?"

"Well, there's this store called Miller's. . . ." I began.

"Miller's, yeah. I know exactly how to get there. But better you should take the subway," she said. "It's, like, an impossible walk."

"The *subway*? Are you kidding? I was told I'd get murdered or something if I took the subway."

"So how are you supposed to get around?"

"By cab," I said. "I promised my husband I'd travel by cab."

"Except look what happened to you," Flora reminded me. "Trust me," she said. "I'll get you to the subway and the subway will get you to Miller's."

"Are you sure you know what Miller's is?" I asked. I mean, I'd had no luck at all with even official sources.

"I told you," she said, "I'm a horse nut myself. I go there all the time. To the bargain basement, usually."

"You mean there really *is* an El Dorado?" I said, but the minute I uttered it, I knew from her puzzled expression that she thought I meant a Cadillac. "There really *is* a bargain basement?" I restated, and she brightened.

"Yep. There really is. Hey, wait a minute, lookit there." She was frowning at a spot on my upper right thigh. "You've got some oil on your pants or something."

"Oh, no!" I strained to see, but the stain was too far to the rear. I was wearing the riding pants I mentioned earlier, the ones that looked like leggings. Actually, it was one of those riding unitards, you know, a one-piece deal. But as I mentioned before, everything that has to do with riding costs a mint. I couldn't afford to have my only riding unitard—we're talking about a hundred bucks here—ruined by some New York City mugger.

"I live right up the street," Flora offered. "We could put some Spray'n Wash on them and run them over to the Laundromat. You have time?"

"I guess," I said.

"Let's do that, then."

While Flora was leading me toward her digs, she began speculating about the woman who'd knocked me to the ground. "What was she doing here?" she said. "I mean, did you see the way she was dressed? Very Upper East Side."

"Upper East Side?"

"You know, matching purse and shoes, Mia suit, that kind of thing."

"Oh yeah? That was an actual Mia suit?" Fashion, as you may have surmised, is not one of my major interests.

"That plaid suit she was wearing, yup. It's a Mia suit. Mia is *the* big designer. Big this year, anyway. You can always tell because of the buttons and the braid. It's not my kind of thing, but I know it when I see it." Then she changed the subject. "So have you read the deKunffy yet or not?"

"I started it," I said. Right. I was on page one.

"I like what he has to say about the training value of the shoulder-in," she said, "as opposed to the leg-yield."

"My God," I shrieked, "you really *are* a horse person. And a dressage person, too."

"What'd I tell you." Flora shrugged. "We probably grew up the same, you and me. Horse pictures all over the wall and stuff."

"I know. But still, dressage!"

Dressage is a pretty esoteric sport. You can hang around with actual horse people and *still* not find someone who so much as knows what it is. How very rare, then, in a city like New York, to find a total stranger who could talk about the training value of leg-yield versus shoulder-in.

A semiwicked smile crept over my face. Jeet, in some publisher's office on the other side of town, was probably feeling a twinge in his chest or an increase in his heartbeat or something as this Stranger-Than-Fiction coincidence was being enacted.

"What's funny?" Flora wanted to know.

"I was just thinking about my husband," I said. "He was really gloating about the fact that there weren't any horses in the city for me to get involved in."

"Ha!" Flora said. "There are about a hundred horses just a block away."

"What!?"

That was when she told me about Claremont. It was where she worked part-time. "It doesn't pay that much," she said, "but I get to ride and be around horses, you know." She shrugged and looked me in the eye. "It matters to me."

She reminded me of that commercial for Sugar Frosted Flakes, you know, a grown-up admitting to indulging in what is thought of as a childish yearning.

"It matters to me, too," I assured her.

Hey, I knew what she meant. In fact, if I lived in New York, I'd do exactly the same. I mean, even if I were married to the highest-paid cookbook author ever, which is of course what Jeet and I were both hoping. The book part, not the NYC part. But the thing is, it matters to a lot of people, grown-up people. And somebody in advertising knows it, too. I mean, is it an accident that there's a horse in all those television commercials for perfume? Or cars? I mean, think about horses for a minute—those great big bodies on little spindly legs. Don't you think they'd be extinct by now if there weren't hordes of us worshiping them? Brushing them, feeding them, picking out their hooves, and painting their hooves with goo. I mean, *I*, who have never had a professional manicure, actually drag myself outside twice a week to paint some sort of petroleum product on my horses' hooves every summer lest they crack or chip or peel. I ask you!

But as usual, I digress. It's pretty much what I was saying while Flora and I walked along for about eight or nine more blocks, though.

Then, out of the blue, Flora asked, "Did you ever read *Heads Up, Heels Down*?"

I was floored. "By C. W. Anderson?" I asked. This book had been the first I'd ever read on the subject of horses. I had taken it out of the library so many times that I'd memorized it, words and drawings both. God, I *loved* that book, and told Flora so.

"Do you remember the drawing of a horse's fetlock—the feathers and everything?"

The fetlock is in the back of the horse's leg right above the hoof, and the feathers are the long hairs that grow there. In show horses these hairs are trimmed, but if you think of the feet on draft horses, workhorses, where these hairs are left intact, you'll probably know what I mean.

"Yes," I said, "I remember." We had stopped walking and I shut my eyes to conjure up the image, which I could do in a pretty detailed way.

"Do you remember what it said? Like the caption?" she asked.

I tried to think.

She gave the answer before I could come up with it. "It said, 'A hairy fetlock is unsightly and can easily be remedied with a pair of scissors.' Well, picture this. After I read that, I used to carry a pair of scissors, you know, the kindergarten kind with the rounded edges, just in case I came upon a horse with a hairy fetlock. I mean, imagine this. In Queens. I was, I don't know, maybe nine years old."

I laughed and recounted my own memory of Anderson's language—which, by the way, introduced me to understatement. "He was writing about getting a first horse and he said to choose a hunter," I said, "because—if I remember it correctly—'should a fence intervene between you and open country, he will solve the problem nicely.' "

"I remember that!" she said.

We started to walk again. "But those drawings," I said. "I can still see them."

"Those soft-eyed foals," she said.

"This is uncanny," I told her. "Like, if it happened in a movie—meeting you, I mean, and you liking horses and knowing dressage and reading C. W. Anderson—it would be too hokey to be true." But it was true. I had met a kindred soul. I wanted to invite her to Primrose Farm, have her get on Plum, and ride over to Lola's with me.

"Do you think that there are little girls everywhere," I asked her, "just like us? Little girls in Japan and Italy and Newfoundland who are looking at horse books and—"

"Not just Japan and Italy," she interrupted me. "But on Pluto and Mars and Jupiter, I'll betcha."

I wanted to introduce her to Wanda.

Finally we came to a doorway between what appeared to be a clothing store and a miniature supermarket. Flora pressed a button on an intercom, and a hollow sound with something resembling a "Yeah?" boomed out.

"Four-three," Flora said, looking up at what I now realized was a video camera. "High security," she said to me, winking. "The fact is, except for Tubular, these guys never look up from the porn mags they're reading."

The door buzzed and Flora pushed on it and we went inside before I could ask about the Tubular part.

It was a staircase, carpeted and clean. On the landing between the street and the lobby floor were a bank of phones. At least a decade's worth of numbers had been scribbled onto the walls. "Like in the old movies, huh?" Flora said.

As we rose, the heat grew thicker, and on four, where Flora evidently lived, it threatened to overwhelm. "That's a drawback," Flora said. "No air-conditioning. But that's the only way I can afford this place. It's called the Farragut, by the way. Classy sounding, huh?"

I smiled. I was trying to picture myself living here as we walked. I was trying to picture a life this incredibly different from my own.

"Are you happy?" I asked Flora.

She turned around and looked at me.

"I don't know," she said, as if she'd never considered it. "I guess so."

Flora shared one of two end-of-the-corridor baths with the other six rooms on the floor. "I come from this big huge family," she explained, "so it's no problem. You have to remember to bring your toilet paper back and forth, though, because leave it in there, and bingo, it's like gone. But other than that . . ." She continued down the hall.

"Where is your family?" I asked.

"Queens."

Her own door had no knob. Still, she needed a key to get into it. It opened onto a single room with a single unmade bed, a sort of cardboard dresser, and a sink. There was a window staring out at yet another window just about an arm's length away. I peered out and down into a litter-strewn passageway several flights below.

"Not a pretty sight, huh?" Flora said.

I didn't answer. I mean, what could I say? Our place

back in Texas isn't *House Beautiful*, by any means, but it was a damn sight better than this.

There was one of those tiny bar-sized fridges and a two-burner hot plate. But Flora was tiny herself. She probably never ate. Even on the shelf above the hot plate, there was nothing to indicate that she did.

She watched me looking around. "Mostly I just sleep here, you know," she explained.

She opened the closet, which was brimful of clothing. On the shelf above the rack where the clothes were hung was a shelf. I could see the spines of big-name fashion magazines: *Marie-Claire* and *Elle* and *Vogue* and *Harper's Bazaar*. She had quite an accumulation of them.

"Guess I like clothes." She smiled in a kind of apologetic way.

I don't know if I'd have noticed what she was wearing otherwise. I mean, I'm ordinarily pretty oblivious to such things. I buy maybe a dress a year, if that, so I'm not exactly keeping the fashion industry hopping. After all, most of my time is spent shoveling horse dung or riding the dungmakers.

Flora was wearing a skirt the size of a washcloth, maybe even smaller, and black fishnet hose. She had paddock boots on with this outfit, you know, the lace-up kind. She'd topped things off with a T-shirt that appeared to be made of velvet or at least velour. I've already mentioned the earrings. She was wearing earrings the size of the chandeliers at the Spanish Riding School in Vienna. For all I know, they were replicas of the chandeliers there.

In my pseudo-leggings and big top, I felt really out of

it, fashion-wise. I said so as I slipped out of first the top and then the unitard. I stood there in my undies and watched as she produced some Spray'n Wash to cover the oil stain.

"There's some jeans and shirts and stuff in the bottom of the closet here that'll fit you," she said, nudging a pile of clothes with her toe and finally freeing something denim, which she moved in my direction.

"No way," I told her. "You're about a third my size." It wasn't much of an exaggeration.

"They're my former roommate's," she said. "He was, um, bigger than me."

They fit perfectly.

We walked around the corner to the Laundromat and I soaked in this first-time-ever feeling of being a New Yorker. Flora, however, seemed fascinated by my life at home. Nobody else had ever seemed fascinated, and I warmed to this, big time, babbling with affection about everything I profess to despise: the heat, the scorpions, the fire ants. I made life at Primrose Farm sound like a Watteau painting.

I laid it on especially thick when I told her about Jeet, saying he was a "semifamous writer."

"Like a journalist, or what?"

"Like a journalist," I answered. "Right."

"An investigative journalist?"

"Well . . ." I thought about Jeet's restaurant reviews. We did go to restaurants anonymously to sample the food and the service and whatnot. That seemed investigative enough. "That's right," I said. "He does this undercover stuff."

"So what's his book gonna be about?"

"It's still pretty hush-hush," I told her. I didn't want to blow my newfound image admitting that my husband was going to be writing about his aunt Nellie's custard and his uncle Festus's fudge and maybe even sharing with his readers his very own recipe for shortcake.

"But what about *your* life, Flora?" I asked her. "You seem to have the best of both worlds. I mean, living here and still able to be around horses."

"Yeah, well, you'll have to come to Claremont tomorrow and ride. You'll be here tomorrow, huh?" She waited until I'd nodded yes and then went on. "Maybe I'll be able to go out with you. You know, around the park."

"Central Park?" My eyes got wide. That was one of the places I was definitely supposed to stay out of. Of course, truth be told, I probably wasn't supposed to follow a total stranger home and strip to my underwear, either, although this had never been specifically vetoed.

"Central Park. Where else?" Flora said.

I wasn't sure what Jeet's plans were, and so I gave her our room number at the hotel and told her to call me.

"Okay," she said, "but listen. Your pants are gonna take a while, so why don't we go down there now."

"And ride, you mean?"

"Well, no, I mean just kind of look around."

"Yeah, sure," I said.

"Except we'll have to sneak in, kind of, because afternoons this guy who hates me, Sellers, is working."

"Oooh," I said. Across town someplace, there was Jeet again, feeling that a pin had been stuck into a voodoo doll with his face on it. Except that it did seem like a very daring way to spend a New York afternoon.

"How will we do that, though?" I wondered. "Sneak in, I mean." Wouldn't security in New York City be primo?

It turned out that whenever Flora couldn't sleep, she'd go down to Claremont and schmooze with the horses. I don't know if you know what barns are like at night, but they're peaceful beyond measure. Just an occasional munch on the hay and a snort here and there. It's relaxation city. Even the sound of mice scurrying about adds to the snugness of it all. So I could understand hanging out in the stable after hours. It made sense to me. Still, how did Flora get in?

"See?" Flora said, holding up a huge key ring shaped like a snaffle bit. "I have this key."

It turns out Flora would come in through a side door in the morning, the first person there, and feed.

"Cool," I said.

The door led directly into a small manège—that's an indoor riding area. It wasn't big the way regulation dressage arenas are big, but it was large enough to accommodate, oh, maybe ten horses in a lesson. There were pillars, though, instead of the huge clearspan spaces I'm used to. But the building was old—a hundred years old, Flora said—so I guess the clearspan era hadn't dawned when it was built. (Still, how old is the Spanish Riding School in Vienna? Or am I in danger of becoming a pedant here?)

But Flora was shutting the side door and telling me to

just act natural. "There's always a mob scene here, so if you just act cool, no one will notice you. But they take a break during the day, and if we're lucky, we'll hit that."

We walked in, and we weren't lucky, but I followed Flora's advice about acting cool, and sure enough, we seemed invisible. Flora led me to a ramp along the side. We walked down. It was covered with canvas. "I know that smell," I said as we descended into one of the stabling areas. Horses—someone said it's because they don't eat meat, and I don't know if that's true or not—smell clean and good.

And sure enough, there they were, row upon row of horses, all of them chowing down on their hay. Mostly these were standing stalls, but Flora told me there were box stalls upstairs.

There was even a blacksmith, full-time, Flora said. "Hey, girls." He called a greeting without really looking up from the shoe he was pounding on.

"This is incredible," I said.

"Wait till you see upstairs," she said.

She said that if we waited until what she called "siesta time," when everyone booked out for lunch or whatever, she would ride a horse she'd been working with. He was one of the beginner horses, a lesson horse, she said, but special. "You know what I mean," she said, and I did.

Still, I couldn't help wondering what you could get out of riding a lesson horse. I mean, lesson horses—at a stable that takes beginners, especially—would be wretched to ride, I thought.

Because horses protect themselves, close themselves

off. Those who have beginners—teachers call these the "up-downs"—bouncing around on them close themselves especially.

A well-trained horse, on the other hand, is usually well ridden and is wide-open, listening to every breath that the rider takes. To a well-trained horse, every movement, every tensing of a rider's muscle, means something.

So why would Flora want to ride a lesson horse?

Of course, I supposed that a lesson horse was better than none.

She put a bridle on the horse and one of those lightweight Wintec saddles. Then she led the horse to the manège, with me on her heels.

The horse, whose name was Sasha, drooped along while led.

Pathetic, I thought.

I found an elevated row of three theater chairs in the corner and climbed into one. I readied myself—a smile affixed to my face, the injunction to *be-nice-no-matter-what!* in my heart.

And then Flora, microskirt and all, mounted.

When she closed her legs around the horse, a miracle happened. You could see the horse go, *I know these legs,* his ears twitching busily. Then: *I love these legs.*

Flora spoke to him with her seat, and his neck arched in response. Flora was doing what Vicky Hearne says dressage does: she was calling forth the horse's beauty.

I felt a thrill shiver through me. This was a horse who was opening himself, a horse who was allowing all of his tactile powers to come into play. He walked out onto the circle, a totally different horse from the one who had come into the manège.

My eyes teared and a huge lump formed in my throat. I wondered where Flora would be right now if she'd been born into a family like mine, a family who schlepped her around to weekly riding lessons and horse shows. Gearing up for the Olympics, maybe.

But then we heard a noise.

"Oh, shit!" Flora said, jumping down, and rushing away with Sasha in tow. "Quick, someone's here."

I scooted down and went running off after her.

She sent Sasha to his stall and she and I began creeping along an aisleway. So far, so good.

We were about to turn a corner when a booming male voice rang out. Even the horses jumped at the sound.

"Who's that?" I whispered.

"Guess," Flora said.

Instinctively, I ducked into one of the standing stalls. There was a big fat pony in there, a dapple gray. He began to frisk me for carrots, moving his nose from jean pocket to jean pocket, then up and down my chest.

"What the hell are you doing here?" I heard the man—Sellers, I was sure—ask Flora.

"I . . . I . . ." she said.

"You're always snooping around," he said. "I don't like it one bit."

"I'm not snooping, I just . . ."

Meanwhile, where I was crouched, the pony flapped his lips and snorted in disgust, probably a response to the fact that I bore no goodies rather than to Sellers and the way he was ranting at Flora. In any case, pony spittle dotted my face and neck.

"Just get out of here," Sellers was yelling.

"But I ..." Flora said. You can see from her responses that she and I had a lot in common.

"Out. Now. Come on." Sellers was evidently marching Flora to the door.

That left me, an interloper, to fend for myself. I remembered, though, what Flora had told me: *Act as though you belong....*

With that in mind, I waited until the voices had receded and began to move toward the section where the ramp was. I had to pass the blacksmith, but, as before, he didn't look up.

Just then a female voice boomed out over a loudspeaker. It sounded like some military code or the things football players shout in a huddle. Incomprehensible. "Dusty," the voice said, "Lancelot, Mecklenburg, and, um, Annie."

Where was the ramp? I had been down so many little aisles that I was totally discombobulated, no sense of direction. I was still blundering around when I saw the horses coming toward me. Oh, they weren't running or anything. They were kind of moseying along. I stood back and they passed me, kind of like horse robots. They were also fully tacked up—saddles and bridles in place, reins looped along their necks.

It dawned on me: they were going to the ramp. So I followed them, and sure enough, they led me right to it. They were—Dusty, Mecklenburg, Annie, and Lancelot—on their way to work.

In full view of everyone—which now included four hard-hatted Asian children dressed in jodhpurs and paddock shoes—I walked out the wide front entrance and onto the street.

I oriented myself and aimed in what I thought was the direction of Broadway. Sure enough, there was Flora, waiting for me.

"Did anybody see you?" she asked.

"Everybody saw me," I said.

"But did anybody say anything?"

"No."

"Awright!" she said, raising her hand at me the way basketball players on TV do at each other when they've made a spectacular play.

"Awright!" I answered, slapping my palm against hers.

By the time my unitard was ready, she and I seemed old friends. I even trusted her enough to let her lead me down a flight of stairs underground into the subway.

"Listen," she said as she put me on the train and told me what street to get off at, "I'll see you tomorrow, okay? I'll call you."

Tomorrow. Were there any rules left for me to break?

CHAPTER 3

"And then we had jambonnette"—Jeet was rhapsodizing about the lunch he'd eaten at some hotshot editor's expense—"and it was fabulous. It was glazed, you know, like a galantine, and—"

"What is that?"

"Galantine? Or jambonnette? Jambonnette is bacon and pork shoulder that's kind of . . ." He began motioning with his hands, as if patting this mixture into a shape.

"Oh, yuck. Stop," I said. Bacon I could handle, but something about the words *pork shoulder* made me want to gag.

Jeet knew my aversion—well, not to meat, exactly, because I ate hamburger and chicken sometimes and, as I mentioned, bacon—but to anything that resembled an animal's musculature. Even so, in all the years Jeet had been reviewing restaurants for the *Austin Daily Progress*, no one seemed to notice that Jeet's companion—because that was how he always referred to me in his articles—had these culinary peculiarities.

"I was going to call you to join us," Jeet said, "but

38

when they said we were going to a place called Charcu-
terie, I knew better. You aren't upset, are you?"

I opened my mouth, but before I could tell him no, he
was off again.

"Oh!" he said, "I didn't tell you about dessert! Now,
that you'd have liked." He closed his eyes for a moment
as if in ecstasy.

"You ought to weigh three hundred pounds," I said
when he was done. And boy, that's true. Why is it men
can eat as much as they do and stay skinny, while we
have only to look at, say, the chocolate cake on the
cover of *Woman's Day* or *Family Circle* to gain three or
four pounds?

He opened his eyes and looked at me. "So what did
you have to eat today?" he asked.

I tried to think. Had I eaten? Oh, right. I'd eventually
gone into a deli and had an egg-salad sandwich. It had
too much mayo in it, but the bread was good and the
dill pickle had been luscious, the kind that snaps crisply
as you sink your teeth into it.

I relayed this info, and Jeet seemed pleased. "A New
York deli," he said. "Good choice. What did you do?
Just walk around until you saw one that looked good?"

The time had clearly come to inject Flora into the
conversation. I knew, though, that he wouldn't approve.
I mean, she was one of the strangers he'd cautioned me
not to talk to.

"Well, I met this girl," I said.

Jeet cocked his head.

"Flora something," I went on.

"Met her where?"

"On the street. I mean, this really well-dressed

woman knocked me down and Flora came and picked me back up."

"Someone knocked you down?" he said. "Where were you?"

I decided not to tell him how far I'd ventured from the hotel. "Right near here," I said. "She might not have knocked me down on purpose," I lied. "I mean, she was dressed really well. Had on this Mia suit." I copied from what Flora had said.

"A Mia suit. That's what my agent was wearing."

"How do you know?" Fashion isn't my husband's thing, either.

"Because someone commented about it. It was plaid and kind of stiff or something, and it had these decorations, I don't know, sort of strips that went down here." He indicated the lapel. "And buttons. Anyway, go on."

But I was laughing. I mean, I had seen a Mia suit. If I hadn't, there would be no way to even begin to imagine the article of clothing that Jeet had described. But like I said, fashion isn't his thing.

"So okay," he said, refusing to let me get off the track this way. "This woman knocked you down and a girl named Flora picked you up."

I abbreviated the tale, not going into the whole stain on the breeches part and the Laundromat part. And not going into the stable part, either. I did, however, make the mistake of telling him I might be going to see Flora again tomorrow, because tomorrow, she thought, we could ride. "She's going to call or come by," I said.

"You told her where we were staying?"

"Well, of course I did," I said.

"Robin, she's probably a crook."

"She's not a crook," I defended her.

"She's probably going to come here tonight and rob us."

"Jeet, you're crazy. All these stories about New York have made you nuts."

"They aren't just stories, Robin," he said. "Jeez. I don't even know if we should leave the room to go to dinner. In fact, we probably should change rooms, that's what. Did you give her our room number?"

I smiled weakly. Before I finished smiling, Jeet was rolling his eyes and calling the desk.

"Don't you realize," he said, "that the woman who knocked you down and this Flora person were probably working together?" He looked at me. "Oh, come here," he said, putting his arms around me and nuzzling my hair. "You're so innocent. That's one of the things I love about you."

I swallowed hard. I'd told him how many lies in the course of the last fifteen minutes?

The people at the hotel said they'd have everything moved to another room and even another floor without our being there, and they didn't seem to think Jeet had gone off the deep end over this at all.

Meanwhile, Jeet kept saying that instead of dinner we ought to stay in our room and guard our possessions.

"You have to do this dinner thing with your agent," I said, astonished to find myself cast into the role of the Rational One. "You can't pass that up just because of some really remote suspicion."

Jeet responded with an incredible catalog of big-city

scams. It was as if he'd been collecting these stories for years.

"Where did you hear all of this?" I asked.

"People back home. Ever since I said we were coming to New York, people back home have been telling me stories."

Jeet ended up calling his agent, Maggie, and she rounded up her husband and the two of them met us in the hotel lobby, even though it was way early by most people's standards to be thinking about dinner.

And they—Jeet's agent, Maggie, and her husband, Ed—seemed to think that Jeet's assumption about Flora and the Mia-suited woman was a hundred-percent correct.

"They were definitely working together," Maggie offered, looking at me. "The woman who knocked you down and the one who picked you up."

"Oh, for God's sake," I said. "Maybe you and Ed are in on it, too. Maybe you're supposed to lure us away from our room. Because then they can have a clear shot at stealing, I don't know, our travel alarm clock. And my nightgown. And God. Let me think. What other precious things do we have up there?"

They both looked puzzled. They looked at each other and then at Jeet. Jeet, of course, knew that I was exaggerating for comic effect, but these two didn't seem to have a clue. "Thank God," I continued, "that I left the tiara at home. I came this close"—I pinched my fingers together and held them up—"to bringing it."

They laughed uneasily.

"It's okay," Jeet said. "She gets this way."

"But . . . but . . ." Since I hadn't told Jeet in the very beginning about following Flora back to her place and washing out my breeches and all, I couldn't very well do so now. But didn't all of that confirm that Flora was a legitimate Good Samaritan and not some thief?

I wanted to set their minds at ease. Maggie's mind and Ed's mind and, especially, Jeet's.

"She works at a riding stable," I tried. "And she knew who Charles deKunffy was."

"Charles who?" Maggie asked. She was thinking Manson, I could tell.

"That proves it," Jeet said. "You don't live in New York City and work in a riding stable!"

"There is one," I whined. "There is."

"Robin—" Jeet started, but Maggie intervened.

"No, there really is," she said, "Claremont. It's on Eighty-ninth Street. They've made movies there. *Marathon Man* and, oh, gee, help me out, Ed. What's that other one?"

"A riding stable," Jeet said. "I should have known." He glared at me as if I'd planned all of this from way back before we left Texas.

"I don't remember a riding stable in *Marathon Man*," I said. "Do you remember one?"

"Maybe it wasn't *Marathon Man*," Maggie said. "But I wish I could remember the name of that other one. These horses tried to trample someone."

"You ought to call the stable," Ed was saying, and Jeet was listening intently. "Just to confirm that this Flora person really does work there."

"Yeah," I said, "do that." This would vindicate my new friend, I was sure.

"I think the word *witness* was in the title. Like, *Eye-witness* or something like that." Ed looked at his watch. "It's still pretty early. If I were you, old man, I'd call Claremont right now."

"Maybe they know which movie," Maggie was saying. "*Witness. Witness.*"

We gathered at a bank of pay phones near the rest rooms.

"Do you know her last name?" Jeet stood with a quarter at the ready.

"Uh, it was something with a B. B . . ." Actually, I couldn't remember if Flora had told me her last name or if I'd seen it on the mailing label of one of the many fashion magazines at her place. "B-E-N . . ." I continued spelling and conjuring at the same time until the name Benavides had been produced.

Jeet dialed.

And minutes later hung up, looking grim. "No such person works there," he told us.

Maggie and Ed and I gasped. Then I got hold of myself.

"Wait," I said, "let me try." I held my hand out and watched as everyone began fishing through pockets. Ed finally placed a quarter in my palm.

So I called Claremont, too, and included a pretty good physical description of Flora. The answer was the same: no such person worked there.

"Satisfied?" Jeet asked me.

What was I supposed to say? That she'd taken me there? And that she had a key? For all I knew, that side door was open all the time. And while it was true that the blacksmith had spoken to us, it was also true that he hadn't used any names. In fact, he hadn't even looked up.

And Sellers, well, of course he would have asked her to leave. She was an intruder, so why wouldn't he? But God! I had to admire the lengths to which Flora had gone to convince me that she was okay.

But this was crazed. Of course Flora worked there. What was wrong with this picture was New York, which had day shifts and night shifts and Lord only knows what all. What was wrong here was that whoever had answered the phone was on a totally different shift from Flora's, so of course that person wouldn't know that she worked there.

There are a million explanations in the naked city.

But meanwhile, Jeet was back to high-level paranoia. "We can't go out now," he was saying. "We just can't."

"Jeet," I tried, "we changed rooms, remember? And I wasn't exactly kidding about having nothing with us that would be worth stealing. I mean, think about it."

Jeet remained unconvinced. Finally, even Ed and Maggie were trying to get him out onto the street.

"Look," I said, "I know where this Flora person lives."

"You do?" They actually chorused it, all three of them.

"That's right," I said.

"But how?" This was Jeet.

"I, uh, saw where she went. After she picked me up. So if we get robbed, I'll just call the police and lead them to her place."

"You know the address?" Jeet asked.

"Not the address, but I know how to get there."

"Let's go there tonight." Maggie's eyes burned. Here was a woman who liked adventure.

Jeet sighed. "No. You're right. I'm getting carried away here." He brightened then. "Let's go eat!"

We walked up the avenue while I pondered all of this. Finally we came to an Indian restaurant, where, as if of one mind, we all sought to drown our sorrows in saag paneer and tandoori shrimp and lassi and such.

The restaurant we chose was cool and comforting, all dark wood and crisp table linens. It smelled of tamarind and incense. Ravi Shankar twanged in the background while handsome waiters in white shirts, black trousers, and maroon turbans bustled about. In other words, perfect.

It was so early that only three tables were occupied. We were at one while a lone woman sat at another. A couple necked at the third, so passionately that I wondered how they'd noticed anything resembling hunger as one ordinarily used the word.

Then, on my way back from the ladies' room, I noticed their plates. The food had barely been touched. The degree of desiccation, however, led me to believe that they had been in the restaurant since noon, ignoring the glances—envious, angry, whatever—that came their way.

The lone woman was as cool as they were hot. In fact, there was something imperious about the way she arched her brows as she studied the menu. Sure enough, she snapped her fingers to summon a waiter and began questioning him about the dal. Was animal fat used in its preparation? she wondered. The use of animal fat was a no-no, she said, only she didn't phrase it this way. What she said was that she found the use of it hideous, and she made herself shiver dramatically to reinforce her statement.

The waiter looked puzzled. "You wait one minute," he said, bowing and backing toward the kitchen. "I find out for you." His voice had that wonderful singsong quality that John Belushi used to parody so brilliantly on *Saturday Night Live* and even before then, in *Lemmings*. But this wasn't enough for the woman.

"I want to know right now!" she said, tossing her napkin onto the tabletop as she stood. She was right out of the pages of *Vogue*, in an evening rendition of the Mia suit, little black braids hanging from its lapels. The woman herself was starkly beautiful: bone thin with the palest skin set off by pitch-black hair that was cut boyishly short.

I looked over at our table, and sure enough, everyone there was staring. Ed looked vaguely embarrassed, while Maggie seemed pleased to have a front-row seat. I looked over at the couple at the other table. They hadn't noticed a thing. They were engaged with each other, exactly as before.

A man in a chef's hat came through a pair of swinging doors, a cloud of steam behind him. "Yes, I can help?" he asked.

"Your waiter," the woman said, "is poorly informed on humane matters," the woman said.

"Humane, yes," the man in the chef's hat said. It was clear that he hadn't a clue. He looked around the room as if to ask for help.

In the background, I saw Jeet making his way toward

her. "Perhaps I can help," he was saying, smiling at the
woman. "I know something about the way Indian food
is prepared. . . ."

Jeet succeeded in making the woman do something
that approximated a smile, but in the end, she got up to
leave the restaurant without ordering.

Suddenly several people came bursting in and the
room lit up with what seemed portable floodlights. A
man with a minicam began interviewing the woman
while she went on and on about the disgusting practices
that preceded the eating of meat.

"Oh, no," I said, holding my ears. I'm as much of an
animal lover as the next person, but enough already. I
had trouble watching *The Texas Chainsaw Massacre*,
and not because of the people being offed by
Leatherface. No. For me, it was all the talk about cows
and the slaughterhouse. I mean, I can't handle it.

"Why can't she just go to a veggie place?" Jeet whispered.

"And so, animal lovers," the man with the cam was
wrapping up, "if Mia eats there, you can be sure—"

"Mia!" Maggie said. "I knew I'd seen her somewhere! It's Mia!"

"Is she done?" I asked, removing my palms from my
ears.

"Why can't she just go to a veggie place?" Jeet repeated.

"Anyone for samosas?" I said hopefully. "And
maybe some bhujias?" Indian food is one thing Jeet
didn't have to teach me. "How about—"

"I should get one of my authors to do a book about
Mia," Maggie went on. "A woman with a cause."

"Meat is my favorite thing," Ed said.

Eventually, they talked publishing while the restaurant filled. I began counting Mia suits—there were a lot of solid-color eveningish ones like the one that the woman had worn, all recognizable by the buttons and the braid—kind of like a querulous kid on a long car trip counting woodies. It occurred to me that Mia had set the whole thing up for publicity, but why? Given the fact that every other woman in New York was wearing something she'd designed, she sure didn't need the exposure. I voiced this.

Then I saw the tooka on Ed's plate. "Aren't you going to eat this?" I asked, with fork poised.

"Some people never get enough," Jeet said.

I thought for a minute he meant me, but then he added, "And it's certainly a popular cause."

At meal's end, the man in the chef's hat appeared again and said he was serving us kheer—rice pudding—on the house. Jeet talked him into a tour of the kitchen, and once again all was right with our world.

CHAPTER 4

"Want us to come back with you?" Ed asked. I could see that Maggie was hoping we'd say yes. But Jeet, his angst assuaged by massive quantities of highly spiced food, was feeling brave.

"Naw," he said. "We've got a handle on it."

Nonetheless, we both grew stealthy, like plainclothes cops embarking on a drug bust, as soon as the elevator hit our floor. Which is to say that Jeet and I tiptoed up the hall to our new room and pressed our ears to the wall and then the door for a good long while.

It was actually kind of fun. And I was amazed by the amount of police procedure that my husband, largely through osmosis since I was the one who watched crime shows, had absorbed.

For instance, the way Jeet inserted the key and jumped back as if expecting gunfire. Finally, veeeerry slowly, he turned the key, turned the knob, and shoved the door, *blam,* back against the wall.

And of course all our stuff was in there, undisturbed.

Nonetheless, I had to watch as Jeet looked out the window (we were now on the eighth floor), under the bed, in the closet, even in the bathtub.

"Think the coast is clear?" I asked. I'd actually toyed with saying, *My hero*, but thought it too sarcastic.

"I think we're safe . . . for now."

"But think about it, Jeet," I tried. "What could they be after?"

"Oh, I don't know, hon," he said in this tortured voice. "I just know that I don't like it. I don't like it one bit. In fact, I'll bet I don't get a wink of sleep tonight, and tomorrow we've got a big day."

Oh? "What kind of big day?" This was the first I'd heard of it.

"The cookbook editor is going to introduce us to some local chefs. It's a tour she's set up."

"So I guess you can say they're sort of courting you." "They" in this case being the publishing house Maggie was hoping Jeet would sign with.

"I guess."

I sighed. I hate attending these food things. It isn't as though I'm an honest-to-goodness athlete. It's just that I have a propensity to eat too much whenever too much is available, and too much is always available at the places where Jeet is expected as a matter of course to go. I mean, I have been to parties and lunches and dinners and dos that you just wouldn't believe. And the fact is, I, just over the past year, managed to winnow myself down to a point where I don't look totally revolting in a pair of formfitting riding breeches. And Jeet saying, "Well, you don't have to gravitate toward the most fattening food on the table," doesn't help one jot or tittle, because willpower has eluded me all of my life and I don't think that at age thirty-six it's going to be magically visited upon me.

But in this case it was more than food. It was that I'd promised Flora I'd try to go riding with her tomorrow, and also that I was dying to ride. I missed it, missed the motion, missed the exchange that goes on between a rider and a horse. How would I spring *that* on Jeet?

Just do it, I told myself. "Well, I can't go with you tomorrow," I said. "I did tell Flora I'd meet her and that's what I'm going to do." I steeled myself for his response.

No answer.

"Jeet?"

A snore.

You guessed it. Mister I-Won't-Be-Able-to-Sleep-a-Wink had fallen into a comalike slumber. I mean, how can men do this? You can have a knock-down-drag-out argument with a man and end up lying there, shaking all over, while he, meanwhile, will be sleeping like a babe. This is yet another difference between us and them, which, like the food thing, is massively unjust.

I plan, when I die, to picket heaven.

Because for what seemed hours, I shut my eyes and tried to drift off. But no such luck. The minute I'd get to where I'd start sinking into sleep, I'd picture a gang from one of those urban survival movies—you know, nose rings and evil intentions—coming up the hallway toward our room. God, you haven't lived until you've lain abed in a New York hotel room waiting to, at any moment, be mayhemmed.

Oh, eventually I dozed, but then, whoosh, my eyes were open. Open in terror, because I'd become aware of movement in the room. I tensed and listened, at first consoling myself that it had to be Jeet padding to the bathroom. Jeet's stentorian breathing right next to me, however, convinced me this was not the case. It sounded like—yes!—someone rifling through the things we'd spread out on the bureau, like our watches and Jeet's wallet and my fox-mask earrings.

Well, if *that's* all they wanted, they were welcome to the stuff, I thought, but even while I thought it, it occurred to me that maybe Jeet had been right after all. That Flora had been a thief, a thief so brazen that it didn't matter that I knew where she lived and I could, after all, lead police to her door.

I lay there considering my options.

Waking Jeet wasn't one of them. I have learned, over the years, to gauge how deeply asleep my husband is by the sound. Jeet was six fathoms down. If I woke him up, he'd get a case of the bends.

It was up to me.

I would ease out of bed, I decided, and shout menacingly—you know, kind of a crazed karate shout. This was what my old high-school gym teacher, Ms. Barr, always advised. At the same time I could snatch up something like the bedside lamp and wield it as a weapon. (Ms. Barr's weapon of choice was a hat pin, which goes to show how old *she* was. I finally went to an antique store and asked to see one, just so I'd know, and I'll tell you, a hat pin is formidable indeed. But I couldn't figure out how I'd carry one, and anyway, I wouldn't have—surely—kept it on my night table at the ready.)

Anyway, with using the lamp in mind, I began sliding my leg ever so slowly over the edge of the mattress. I had already vetoed the karate shout as too extreme. I mean, it was, probably, the middle of the night.

The rustling continued. I'd catch whoever it was right in the act.

I slid, I slid, I slid until my foot was on the floor. Then I grabbed for the lamp even as I pulled the cord that powered it to illuminate the room and its intruder.

And there I was, face-to-face with a terrified mouse who had been rummaging around on the surface of the bureau. It sat up on its hind legs and chittered, the tiny black beads that were its eyes riveted upon my own.

I don't know about you, but I'm afraid of mice. Oh, not while they are standing still, but when they get moving. And this mouse was ready to do just that. Oh, I know they're tiny, and I know they're timid, but they are also very fast, and when they run around, they scare the bejeesus out of me. I don't know what it is. It's as though I think they're coming for me. And it doesn't matter that I don't know what they'd do when they got me, it just matters that they're coming.

The mouse shook.

I shook.

And then the mouse took off, running in circles around Jeet's wallet and my earrings and the other stuff he'd been rooting through.

My reaction was involuntary. I screamed as though Jack the Ripper had just come in with a pickax. *"Aaaayeee!"*

"Whaa ... what the ..." Jeet sat bolt upright.

I screamed again, and the mouse took a flying leap off the bureau and landed somewhere on the carpet.

I leaped up on the bed, the lamp falling to the floor,

breaking, and hurtling Jeet, the mouse, and me into utter darkness.

In the hall I could hear the sound of slamming doors, muttered curses, and running feet.

"Is it them?" Jeet was shouting. "Are they here?"

"You okay in there?" Someone was pounding on the door. "You okay?"

I was blubbering. "There's a mouse," I said.

Jeet sighed disgustedly and planted his feet on the floor.

"Watch out," I cautioned him. "He's running around."

The overhead light went on, and Jeet blinked at me. His hair looked as if he'd punked it.

Of course by this time, the mouse was long gone.

"Hey. You people all right in there?"

Jeet opened the door. "It's fine. My wife just saw a mouse."

"Yeah, well, how do I know that," a man said.

"Because ... because ..." Jeet is not too swift for about a half hour after waking up. Especially if he wakes up suddenly. I heard him say, "Oh, for God's sake."

He flung the door open, as wide as it would go.

A burly man in striped pajamas looked at me.

"Satisfied?" Jeet asked him.

The man nodded that he was, said, "Can't be too careful," and Jeet slammed the door.

Jeet let out a second sigh of disgust, flicked the light off, and got back into bed. "He didn't believe you were all right," he explained. Then he pulled the blanket over his head.

I got up and flicked the light back on.

"Put the light out," he said, "and get back in bed."

I eased back under the covers.

"Robin . . ." Jeet said. How he could know the light was on with the covers over his head like that is beyond me.

"Mice won't come out if the light's on," I told him.

"Robin . . ."

"Well, okay." I stomped over to the switch, then lay tense and listening. "This is a three-star hotel," I complained. "If a three-star hotel has mice, what would a one-star hotel have?"

"Rats," Jeet said.

I couldn't tell if it was an answer to my question or a general comment on the situation.

I opened one eye. A shaft of sunlight was coming through the place where the two sections of opaque draperies were supposed to meet. Said shaft bisected my face.

I rolled over and pulled the covers over the back of my head. I felt the bed sag. Then the damp presence of my newly showered husband. "If you're not going to do this lunch thing with me today, you'd better have breakfast," he said.

"Mmm-hmm."

"We could have breakfast downstairs," he continued.

"Mmm-hmm."

"Or we could call room service," he said.

"Oh, God," I said. "You aren't still thinking about people breaking in here."

"No," he said. He was smiling, though. "I'm thinking

of facing all of the people on this floor who will be staring at us when we come out of the room."

"Staring at us? Why?" And then I remembered. "Oh," I said.

Jeet was shaking his head at me. "I don't see why you're afraid of mice when you aren't afraid of horses."

"Nor am I afraid of gangs of crooks who prey on tourists," I said, sitting up and stretching.

"Okay, so I was wrong," he said. "But you'll have to admit, the circumstances were suspicious."

"That's because you weren't there," I said. "If you'd actually met Flora, you wouldn't have been suspicious at all."

I waited for a response, but instead heard Jeet dial room service. What followed was Jeet's half of an argument about eggs Florentine, which supposedly was the hotel restaurant's claim to fame. Jeet seemed to be losing.

And sure enough, the next thing I felt was the rush of cold air as the covers were untimely ripped from my person. "We have to go downstairs for the eggs Florentine," Jeet said testily. "Their preparation is—and I quote—'too fragile for room service.'"

"Oh, come on," I said, "be lenient." I was moving toward the bathroom, thinking how easily a culinary crisis could replace thoughts of being mortified. Or thoughts of being robbed, maimed, or killed. "I can just imagine how upset you'd be if they came congealed to the plate with tepid hollandaise."

"It's easy enough to keep hollandaise from . . ."

I turned the water on full blast and so didn't, in this instance, benefit from Jeet's vast store of expertise.

* * *

Less than an hour later Jeet and I were facing each other across an elegantly clothed table in a patch of lace-filtered sunlight.

Everywhere around us was the sound of clinking cutlery and conversation. That, and the smell of cinnamon and yeast breads and coffee.

"Doesn't look like the sort of place where rodents prowl the rooms at will," I offered. "Unless he was a trained mouse, sent to get your wallet. Ha! Think of that! A gang who—"

Jeet hadn't been listening. He said, "Oooh, listen to this," and began to read from the menu. " 'Benedict Arnold.' " He laughed at this. "It's eggs Benedict without the Canadian bacon. They use a slice of tomato instead of meat. Cute."

This is what marriage is all about. Cross-conversations, where the you-say and the he-says don't exactly match up. I was about to share this observation when I glanced through the window onto the street.

And saw Flora with a very determined expression on her face.

Flora was definitely up to something. She kept glancing over her shoulder as she passed through my line of vision toward, I presume, the entrance to our hotel.

She wasn't—according to the plans we'd made— supposed to come here. She was going to call.

So maybe Jeet and Maggie and Ed had been right after all.

". . . And the lady will have—" Jeet was telling our waiter.

"Nothing," I interrupted, sliding out of my chair. "I have to go to the bathroom," I whispered in Jeet's ear. "Emergency."

He and the waiter watched me rushing off in that direction.

When I glanced back, I saw that they'd returned to the business at hand. So I moved past the rest room toward a staircase.

I heard banging as I neared the floor that had been ours before our room had been changed. And sure enough, when I opened the fire door, there was Flora, beating with both hands on the door to our old room.

Would a thief, I wondered, knock?

Before I could seriously ponder this question, the door to our old room opened and an undershirted man wiping shaving cream from his face appeared.

He smiled in appreciation when he saw Flora in her teeny skirt with her frizzy hair and her massive earrings.

"You must be Jeet," she said. "Is Robin here?"

"I must be who?" His eyes traveled down her body in an obvious way.

Flora stepped back, cocked her head, put her hands on her hips. I couldn't see her face, but her entire body took on an air of belligerence.

"How much?" the man asked.

"Robin obviously isn't here," she said, her voice curling in disgust. "I can sure see that. God. You sure are a winner."

The man reached out and grabbed her puny upper arm. "Get in here," he said. "I don't have time for games."

Flora shrieked. "I'm gonna tell. I'm gonna tell your wife, that's what. You hear me?" She was pulling back and wriggling around as she spoke, and she broke the man's hold just as three doors along the corridor popped open.

By this time I had reached her side.

"Oh, Robin, I'm sorry." She collapsed against me. "But it's probably better you should know what a creep he is."

I heard several loud *tsk*s before all of the doors—four, if you include the one she and I were in front of—slammed shut.

"Know that who's a creep?" I asked.

"Jeet." She straightened and shrugged. "I guess you do know. Gee whiz." She waved her hand around, shook her head as if accepting some cold and ugly truth. "I'm sorry. Oh, God, I'm sorry." And she started to cry.

The door opened again and the man waved a couple of bills in our faces. I couldn't see the denominations. "How much for the both of you?" he asked.

I heard whispering behind me and I turned to see two old ladies in bathrobes at a door that had evidently opened very quietly indeed. One was explaining to the other, in a very loud voice, that Flora was a hooker and that I, evidently, was the madam.

"Oh, so young, too," the one receiving this information said, marveling. "Both of them."

Flora pointed at the man with the money. "Is this your husband?" she asked.

"My husband? No way."

"Okay," she said, and then she backed the guy with

the money into the room. "There's no amount of money you could pay either one of us, dickhead," she screamed. "No amount on earth."

"What's she saying?" the deaf old woman asked her friend.

"Something about the money," the interpreter offered.

I stared at them. I continued to stare until the women began to look sheepish. They finally backed into their room and very quietly shut the door.

"Ow!" the man shouted, and then Flora emerged.

"You're a hooker," I said, pointing at her.

"You're a madam," Flora said, pointing at me.

We laughed.

"What are you doing here?" I asked her, once we were able to speak.

"Oh." She started crying again. "Let's go someplace and talk." She gestured toward the door. "Did I get the room number wrong?"

"It's a long story," I said. I led her to the fire stairs and proceeded to tell her all about Jeet's suspicions and how we'd changed rooms.

"Makes sense," she said. "I mean, you can't be careful enough, you know?"

"But that doesn't answer the question," I said. "If you aren't here to rob us, why are you here?" I stopped walking because, on the teensiest off chance she was going to rob us no matter what she said, I didn't want to lead her to our real floor.

I'm not as dumb as people sometimes think.

Flora sighed deeply and sank into a sitting position right there on the metal stairs.

She'd been terminated, she said, by Sellers. "No explanation," she said, "just boom. And I've been living paycheck to paycheck, you know, so that would be bad enough. But that's not all. That's not the worst part.

"The worst part was that I sneaked down there—you know, to Claremont—late last night, you know, to kind of say good-bye to the horses. And listen, Robin, there was something really, really weird."

"What?" I sat beside her.

"I don't know if I should tell you," she said. "I just have the feeling that knowing this is dangerous. But believe me, it's—"

"If you aren't going to tell me," I said, "why did you come?"

She looked at me a long time. "I don't know. Because sometimes you don't know who you can trust except that, I don't know, I know I can trust you. I do. I trust you."

I was moved by what she said. I lowered my eyes, because I felt them tearing up.

"Anyway," she went on, "I went back again this morning, you know, to get my check? Because I, like, need the money. And this Sellers guy, he kind of stands in front of me like he's going to mow me down with his body and he says he'll mail me the check.

"And see?" she continued. "That's not good enough. Because, like, you walk away and you wait for the check to come in the mail and it, like, never does. And then next thing you know, you're out on the street."

That still didn't explain why she'd come to see me. In fact, considering the extremity of her position, it seemed *more* odd that she would. But there wasn't any

way to ask her in the middle of this sad, sad tale, and
so I let her go on.

"So anyway, I had to do something to collect, so I,
like, threatened him, you know?"

"You threatened him?" I asked it with admiration, because Flora is so very small.

"I don't mean with my fists or anything," she said. "I
threatened to, you know, expose him."

"Expose him."

"Well, I meant about the check, but I think he maybe
thought I meant the tails." She hesitated. "Anyway, I
kinda, you know, used your husband."

"Jeet?" And what had she meant, "the tails"? But one
thing at a time.

"Yeah, well, you said he was a writer, so I told this
Sellers guy, 'Hey! I got a friend, Jeet Vaughan, who's a
big-shot investigative journalist for the newspapers, and
I'm gonna tell him what you're up to. I'm gonna tell
him and he's gonna expose you and this little operation
of yours, see?' "

"And what did he say?" I asked.

"He said, 'Oh, yeah?' and I said, 'Yeah,' and he said,
'We'll just see about that.' Anyway, ever since then, I
have been feeling, I don't know, really weird."

"Really weird how?" I mean, it would be hard to
imagine, in this context, what really weird might mean.

"Well, when I got back to my place," Flora said, "the
door was open. I didn't go in, because they might still
be in there, whoever it was, but I thought it was, like,
related."

"So you came here," I said. How do I get mixed up
with paranoid people? I'm a pretty laid-back person,

when you think about it. I mean by comparison with those around me.

"Right," she said. "I came here."

I shut my eyes, the better to think about this. "I'll tell you what," I said at last, deciding that she had to be honest. "Let me take you up to our room and you can wait there." I stood up and watched as she did the same. "Then I'll go over to the stables and see what I can see. But the thing is, I have to deal with Jeet first. So if you can stay here until I do—"

"Deal with him?"

"I mean get him on his way. I mean, he'd be upset if he knew you were here. I don't mean that the way it sounds, but he would be."

She nodded, but I could see she didn't get it.

"Look, Flora. If he knew I was getting mixed up in somebody else's problem, he'd be very upset. Because I do that, I get mixed up in things. And if he knew *he* was mixed up in something"—because Flora had, after all, used Jeet's name—"then believe me, all hell would break loose. So you wait here while I make sure the coast is clear and then I'll come get you, okay?"

This seemed reasonable.

But then, on one of the floors below, the door creaked open. That was when Flora grabbed hold of my hand. I don't think that I knew the full extent of her fear until then. Because even with her tiny little hands, she practically cut off all my circulation with the way she was squeezing.

"What?" I whispered.

"Shhh," she said.

We waited, both of us holding our breath as the foot-

steps of the person neared our landing. I could feel
Flora trembling, and I felt, well, the way I do when a
horse is freaking out. Like the Dispenser of Confidence
and Consolation. I could even imagine myself crooning,
"Easy, easy," the way I do when Plum or Spier is about
to freak. But the thing is, *her* fear was infectious. I
could practically hear my heart banging at my chest,
and I had glommed onto her in pretty much the same
desperate way that she'd glommed onto me.

Finally we were able to see the person to whom the
footsteps belonged. A perfectly benign older woman in
a jogging suit.

Which would have been okay if she—the older
woman—hadn't blanched and tsked and averted her
eyes as she passed us.

Well, what else *would* you think if you encountered
two women huddled up together in a stairwell?

Lesbos, right? I said this to Flora and it effectively
defused her fear. I could feel her trying not to laugh. I
tried, too, but it was useless. Before the woman was out
of earshot, we were whooping and guffawing, Flora
punctuating her laughter with cries of, "Oh, shit! Oh,
shit, I don't believe this!"

When I left her there, I wasn't sure someone else
wouldn't come along to scare her half to death. Still, I
knew that I had to.

CHAPTER 5

"Maybe you're coming down with something," Jeet said, regarding the bathroom emergency I'd feigned in the restaurant. All told, I had been gone from the breakfast table something like twenty minutes, but that was enough to worry Jeet. He'd scarfed his food and come back to the room so fast that I'd barely beaten him there.

"Maybe," I said.

"And the fact that you didn't want breakfast . . ." he speculated aloud. I nodded solemnly. I admit, my turning down food was rare. Especially something with hollandaise sauce on it—an addiction to which, I might add, is probably as deadly as an addiction to heroin or Johnnie Walker Red.

"I wouldn't be surprised if you were coming down with something." Jeet frowned. "This New York air is probably swarming with all kinds of bugs."

"Probably." Though how someone from Austin, Texas, which is the allergy capital of the world, could say such a thing is beyond me. I'm not kidding. All of the allergens float around on belts or something and Austin is the place where these belts converge. In Austin and nowhere but Austin, people get strange ailments like "cedar fever," which I thought was made up until I caught it myself. Cedar fever makes you ache all over, like flu. And if you really have it bad, your throat hurts and your head pounds, too.

"But damn!" Jeet said. "I hate to see you miss the tour of chefs. I wonder if I can get them to postpone it?"

You'll recall that by the time I screwed my courage up enough to tell him that I wasn't going to go, he'd fallen asleep.

"Oh, don't," I said. "Not on my account. I just need to be, uh, near a bathroom."

Jeet's brow began to furrow—the classic look of suspicion—and I held my breath. "That deli you ate in yesterday," he said. "What was the name of it?"

"Oooh, that might be it," I said. "Except I don't know what it was called." That was true.

"Well, where was it?"

I shook my head. "Beats me."

Jeet sighed and asked me a lot of questions, like, did I see spots in front of my eyes? Finally he let it go. "Okay. Drink lots of water," he said, "and maybe have room service send up some ginger ale. And maybe some Kaopectate."

The thought of that combination made my stomach reel, enabling me to, at least fleetingly, look genuinely pained.

"I feel so guilty, though," Jeet said as he slid into his jacket. "I'll be dining like Henry the Eighth, while you'll be stuck here—"

"Don't worry about it," I told him, grateful for the chance to seem noble. "I'll be fine."

I'd wait until the elevator whooshed shut, I decided, and then hie it down the staircase to where I'd left Flora.

Except that Jeet paused. He was thinking over the notion that thieves might still be headed our way, I could tell. And now they'd pry the door to the room open and what should they find but me.

"Not a chance," I reassured him even before he could voice this. "They'd have come by now. Of course, if you're really worried, you could hire Kevin Costner to baby-sit me." I actually hadn't seen *The Bodyguard*, but neither had Jeet, so as a joke it ought to work.

And it did. Jeet chuckled and shook his head at his own idiocy and eased himself into the corridor.

"Morning," I heard Jeet say. Evidently one of our hall mates was out there. But whoever it was didn't reply. Probably the guy who thought Jeet had done something awful to me in the middle of the night to have made me scream.

I'm not an easy person to be married to, I guess.

Just to be on the safe side, I didn't rush right down to Flora. I not only waited for the elevator to push off, but opened one of the windows and leaned way out, trying to spot my husband from eight floors up.

The street was thronged, and even though I was able to locate a stream of folks merging with the masses from what had to be the main entrance to our hotel, I couldn't distinguish Jeet from the others.

I'd never actually seen Jeet from this angle, I realized. I contented myself with a brief and informal count of men exhibiting male-pattern baldness, the tonsure that comes to so many with age.

Flora was huddled into a little mesh-stockinged ball by the time I reached her side. Evidently, she'd heard my footsteps and feared the worst. "Flora," I said, "what on earth do you think is going to happen to you?"

"I don't know," she said, "but it won't be good." She made a gesture at her throat, as if cutting it.

"You really believe that, don't you?" I was incredulous. I mean, everybody always accused *me* of leaping to the worst possible conclusion. Even I wouldn't carry on about something like this. Flora was delusional. And paranoid. Didn't the two usually go together? And weren't they a major mental illness, like listed in the diagnostic manual or something? And hadn't one of the folks warning me about New York mentioned the crazies who were openly roaming the streets?

As if to confirm this, Flora reached up from the spot where she had been cowering and grabbed onto me as if I were a life preserver.

I cast an involuntary glance around for the old lady who had seen us in a similar pose earlier.

"Flora, listen. Let's go upstairs and talk about this, all right?"

She nodded and stood. "Well," she said, "for starters, they're gonna screw me out of my paycheck. That much I know for sure. And the tails," she went on. "That has to mean something."

"Okay," I said, once we'd gotten back to the room, "what's this about tails?"

Flora fished in her bag. "Oh, Robin," she said as she dumped the contents out on the bed. "I hope I'm not signing your death warrant."

She unfolded two newspaper articles. Both were about mutilation of horses—specifically, about the removal of their tails. One case had taken place in Connecticut and another in New Jersey, where, according to the article, people had emerged on Christmas morning to find horses standing in various pastures with their tail hairs shorn.

I looked at these. They were sad, sure, but sad things happen. Some prankster had gone around doing this, thinking it was funny, but that didn't mean it was a trend.

She *is* crazy, I thought.

"Wait a minute," she said, rooting around and producing a Xerox of an article about some textile manufacturer in Somerset, England, who was weaving horsehair into upholstery fabric on a loom.

"All of this stuff is making a comeback," Flora said. "That's why they need the tails." She pointed at a line in the article that talked about the length of a horse's tail determining whether or not it could be used. "I'm telling you, this is happening. It's happening and—"

She started to lose control again, and I took her hand and squeezed it. Maybe she was right. Crazier things have happened, crazier and meaner things, too. Things I didn't want to think about, like the way Premarin, the estrogen drug that postmenopausal women take, is made from mare urine in Canada. They impregnate the mares and stick them in little tie stalls and attach catheters to them to get the urine, and as soon as the foals are born, they're taken and sold to slaughter and the mares are impregnated again. It's ugly, the kind of thing you want to pretend doesn't exist.

"Okay," I said. "I'll go to Claremont and check this out. Meanwhile, don't answer the phone and don't answer the door, all right?" I wasn't exactly sure why, but I remembered that these very injunctions were always issued in detective movies.

Flora nodded. If she was a movie buff, they probably sounded reassuringly familiar to her, too.

"But listen, Flora, are you sure those tails weren't just tied up? You know, like in mud knots?" Mud knots help keep horses' tails clean after they've been washed.

Flora shook her head no. She wasn't looking at me. She was at the window, gazing down into the street as though expecting someone to be out there preparing to storm the building. "It isn't that they're missing. I don't mean they're missing. Not the Claremont horses. What I mean is . . ." She began to get upset and stopped talking. In fact, she started that kind of hiccuping that people do when they're trying not to cry and the tears are forcing their way out anyway.

I took her by the shoulders and led her over to the bed and sat her down. "You'll be safe here," I said. "Jeet will be gone all day. Now refresh my memory and tell me how I get to the riding stable from here."

Directions in hand, I began walking up Broadway. Once again, the New York pace—just on the edge of speedwalking—thrilled me. If you'd asked me right then if I'd give up being a country mouse for this, I'd have said yes.

It occurred to me, too, that those who live in New York City are probably so much healthier than us country folk. Because here, people do actually walk. In the country, you almost never do. You drive everywhere, even down to your own mailbox sometimes. No kidding, we all do this, even though it's only at the end of the drive. And Texas cities—well, Austin, anyway, which is the only Texas city that I really know—aren't made for walking. Half the time there aren't even sidewalks. And drivers—I've done it myself—react with suspicion and even downright hostility toward anyone walking on the roadway.

People dress to walk in New York City. I mean, they'll be in their business clothes, but they'll have Reeboks and Nikes on their feet.

Me, I had paddock shoes. Now granted, they're trendy enough—you know, they're sort of leather hightops that you lace—but they aren't exactly made for pounding the city pavements.

In other words, I hadn't gone very far when my feet began to hurt.

I stopped into a coffee shop and, though tempted by the bagels and doughnuts and wedges of pie, ordered just coffee. While I was sipping it I thought about Jeet. I thought about what he'd say if he knew that I'd stashed Flora, unattended, in our room. And what he'd say if he knew that I was on my way to Claremont to see if the horses had tails. Or actually—considering how delighted he'd been with the notion that there wouldn't *be* horses in New York City—the fact that I was on my way to a stable at all.

* * *

When I got to Broadway and West Eighty-ninth I knew I was at the intersection where the woman in the Mia suit had knocked me down and hijacked my cab. But it was otherwise just a city intersection, with no hint that there were horses just a couple of blocks away.

But had Flora steered me right?

Because these were all *buildings*, right? Buildings, not barns. City buildings, three or four stories tall at least, buildings housing drugstores, shoe stores, clothing stores. I guess I'd been babbling so much when we'd gone there the first time that I hadn't really paid attention to where we were.

But then I caught a whiff of horse manure.

Horse manure. There's nothing offensive about it. I mean, I know people who've grown up in cold places who swear that when they dismount in freezing-cold weather, they head right for the manure pile and stand ankle-deep in the stuff. I mean, who'd ever do that with dog dung? And it isn't just that horse manure doesn't stick to your shoes, either. It's that horse manure doesn't stink. Not that I'm making potpourri out of the stuff, you understand. It's just that when you catch a whiff of horse manure, you don't recoil and say, "Oh, yuck," the way you do when you catch a whiff of other animal droppings.

I mentioned once before that horses smell so good, allegedly, because they don't eat meat. And this, too, is why their manure smells relatively inoffensive. But that can't be the case. I mean, cows don't eat meat either, and have you ever taken a look at their manure? No way anybody would deliberately stand in it. And it does stick to your shoes, too.

I once had this horse-manure conversation with my best friend, Lola, in the presence of a woman who excused herself, saying, "I have always regarded people who are fascinated by the toilet habits of animals with distaste." I mean, that isn't what you're thinking, is it? Because I'm not fascinated, after all; I'm just talking about this because, here I am, walking up a paved city street and I'm smelling horse manure, and you have to admit, that's something!

And sure enough, there I was.

There are about five students in the little manège going around and around—greenies, I can tell, who are maybe just starting to post—and an instructor sitting on an elevated chair that looks like something you'd sit in while having your shoes shined.

But the thing is, the horses these kids are riding all have tails.

"Can I help you?"

You'd think I'd have decided on a strategy before coming here, but I hadn't. I knew that I didn't have to sneak around, though, because no one had seen me here with Flora yesterday. So now I'm torn between saying that I want a job and saying that I want to ride.

"Can I help you?" the young woman repeats.

"I, uh, would like to get a job here. Maybe exercising or something."

The woman laughs like she hears this all the time. And she probably does. I mean, I can't tell you how many times people have offered to "exercise" my horses. Usually these are people who've maybe ridden a couple of years but who gave it up and, discovering that I've got horses, decide, hey, they'll take it up again. Little do they realize that I have horses so that I can exercise them myself. That, plus I would never want my horses exercised by people who thought so little of the sport that they abandoned it.

"Our horses get plenty of exercise," the woman says. She still looks friendly, though.

"Well, I could, uh, groom. Or feed. Or groom *and* feed. Or maybe do tack." But even as I'm talking I'm thinking, What if they hire me? How will I explain this to Jeet?

"I don't think so," she says. "I don't think they're hiring."

"Oh, no? Well, a friend of mine just got fired from here," I said. "Flora Benavides. So you must need someone." God, I don't know what gets into me sometimes. I mean, really.

The woman shrugged and showed me her empty hands, a gesture meaning there was nothing she could do.

"Did you know Flora?" I persisted.

"I'm new here myself," she admitted.

I felt a presence behind me. It was a feeling of menace, as though the temperature had dropped or something. I turned to look, but before I could even accomplish that, the presence spoke.

Not to me. To the woman who had asked if she could help me. The woman looked mildly alarmed.

"You go on, kid," the presence said. "I'll take care of this."

You can guess who it was.

There was my heart again, *ka-thump, ka-thump*. Until now, I was certain that no one had seen me yesterday. Now that certainty began to dissolve. I could imagine myself at the bottom of a compost heap.

I tried to smile. Even though I couldn't see myself, I knew what I had on my face. It was the look that combined both guilt and apology, the look that Kurt Vonnegut once described as a shit-eating grin.

"Okay, so what's the problem?" he asked me.

He was big and beefy, exactly what I *don't* like in a man. He made me feel small and breakable. And also, my neck already ached, what with my head tilted up at an outrageously steep angle.

"I'd like to ride," I said. "I want to rent a horse."

This was Sellers. Sellers, the ogre who had routed poor Flora yesterday. Sellers, who, according to Flora, had not only fired her, but was also going to cheat her out of her pay.

"I thought you said you wanted a job." He was already standing too close to me for comfort. Now he moved in yet another step.

"Well, I did," I said, "but since you don't have any . . ."

Was it my imagination, or did even the horses in the lesson seem more tense with this guy around? I mean, they had been trotting around, perfectly spaced, then *wham!* One of them was now cantering, and another, despite repeated blows to the side by its rider, had broken into a walk. The kids on their backs seemed discombobulated, too. "Everybody walk," the instructor was saying, and the horses responded immediately to the spoken command, as school horses will do. The one that had been cantering slowed so abruptly that the kid in the saddle ended up on the horse's neck.

I tittered when the child herself did.

Sellers did not. He just grumped at me. Some spokesman for the stable, huh? "You need an appointment to ride," he said. He looked around, as if to see if anyone had overheard him.

"Oh. How about if I make an appointment?" I actually hadn't a clue when or if I could get back here, but I was getting, I don't know, belligerent. There was something about him that called up this "Oh yeah?" response in me. This is a major personality flaw that I have thus far been unable to overcome.

"The office is over there," he said, pointing to a walled-off section of the arena. I could feel him watching me as I walked through the dirt to get to it.

Meanwhile, I could see him questioning the girl I'd been talking to.

The office was grimy, but what could you expect with all that dirt being stirred up just a few feet away? There was a sign posted and the prices were listed there. It was steep, but not as steep as I'd feared. An hour's rental, in fact, could be had for thirty-three dollars.

And Sellers was wrong. It turned out I could get on a horse right away.

"How many do you have here?" I asked. I couldn't remember how many Flora had said, but it doesn't hurt to have points of comparison.

"I don't know for sure," the woman said, "but a lot."

She was wearing a headband that had her name woven into it: Tess.

"A lot, meaning what? Twenty? Thirty?"

Tess laughed. "More like a hundred, probably."

"A hundred!"

"Everybody's surprised, but it's true. There are horses in the basement, and horses on all the floors. The building's full of horses."

Well, maybe I am fascinated by the toilet habits of animals at that. Because all I kept thinking of was the manure problem. I don't know if you know about horses, but they produce massive—I mean *massive*— quantities of manure. I'm talking volume. And it never stops coming. Like, if you had to walk a horse the way you have to walk a dog in the city, say, to get it to poop, you'd be walking probably twenty miles a day, three times an hour or something. So what did they do with the manure here? They would need a dump truck every day, probably, to take care of it.

"Do you know the way around the reservoir?" she asked.

"The what?"

"The reservoir. You know, in the park."

"I know nothing," I said. "I've never been to New York before in my life."

"I can get someone to go with you, if you like," Tess said.

"Like who?" I was thinking of how unpleasant it would be to ride with Sellers.

"Like, uh . . ." Tess seemed to be marching people by in her mind's eye, trying to choose one.

"I was supposed to go with my friend. Maybe you

know her. She used to hang out here or work here or something." I looked to see where Sellers was. "Her name is Flora Benavides."

Tess looked at me and frowned. "Name doesn't ring any bells. But hey, I know. I'll go with you."

"Cool," I said.

I looked out into the manège. The kids had all dismounted and were dutifully running their stirrup irons up on the stirrup leathers. My heart warmed to the continuity of all of this. I remembered my first riding teacher, Willy Wines, teaching me this practice. It's something riders automatically do the minute they get off. It's how you can tell, really, whether the rider knows anything or not. Without actually seeing him ride, I mean.

I leaned toward the woman. "Is that big man out there named Sellers?" I asked.

"How did you know?"

She handed me a clipboard and I filled out a form that asked for my name, address, level of riding, and so on. It also asked that I sign a release in case I was maimed, killed, or worse.

I was just finishing up when Sellers came into the office. I was handing the clipboard back to the woman behind the counter when he stepped up and took it out of my hands.

"You're from Texas." He narrowed his eyes. "So what's this about wanting a job?"

"I'm relocating," I said.

"Write down your local address."

"I don't have an address yet. I'm staying at a hotel."

He rolled his eyes. "Write down the name of your

hotel. Room number. Et cetera. We need that." He handed the clipboard back to me.

"Why?" Something was telling me not to do it.

"Why not? You wanted a job, didn't you? So how are we supposed to contact you?"

"But I thought you didn't have any jobs."

He smiled. "Somebody around here could drop dead," he said. "Then we'd have an opening, wouldn't we?"

I wrote the name of the hotel and the room number, but at the same time I thought of Jeet's reaction to my giving Flora all of this information. I mean, Flora wasn't a thief, but who knew about this Sellers character? He was stealing Flora's pay, wasn't he? At least according to Flora. And maybe he was stealing horses' tails as well.

He read what I'd written and tossed the clipboard over the counter to the woman. "She can ride Deadly," he said.

"Deadly?" Tess and I asked it in unison.

I don't know. I was hoping for something with a more neutral name. Or maybe even a name that was benign. Like Serenity or something.

"Deadly Duel," he said.

"Oh." Again, Tess and I spoke as if we'd rehearsed. But hearing the horse's whole name made me feel a lot better.

The woman spoke into a sort of intercom. Then she picked up a hard hat and walked around the counter.

"Where are *you* going?" Sellers asked.

"She doesn't want to be in the park by herself," Tess explained.

"Oh, yeah?" He looked at me. "Why not?"

I felt very small. "Because I'm chicken?" I tried.

This actually made him smile.

Which emboldened me. "Plus I don't know my way around. I'll get lost," I said.

"I'll handle this," he said to the woman. "You stay here."

Sellers was a giant. He would need a horse the size of the Taj Mahal. Plus he was red-faced and fat, obviously out of shape. Nonetheless, he walked behind the desk and went for the intercom. "Bring me Lars," he ordered.

I walked out into the now empty manège. I heard clomping off to my right. A chestnut horse, fully tacked up, the reins looped along its neck, was making its way down a ramp. It walked over to a mounting block, looked at me, and sighed.

"Deadly, I presume," I said, walking over and stroking its neck before mounting.

I was adjusting the length of my stirrup leathers when I heard, not clomping, but booming. This time it wasn't a horse coming *down* the ramp, it was a mega-horse coming *up* from below.

It was Lars.

Who must have been eighteen hands at least. No kidding, think Budweiser hitch here. And he probably did have a lot of Clydesdale in him, too.

Not that I'm not used to big horses. After all, dressage is my thing, and dressage horses are usually plenty big.

Of course, he looked normal once Sellers had climbed aboard him.

"Ready?" Sellers asked, and led the way into the street.

Yes, street. Because that's what we had to do, traverse a busy Manhattan street in order to get to Central Park.

"Wait a minute," I said, clutched by fear. "I'm not sure I'm up to this."

"What do you mean?" Sellers asked, not even looking back at me. "Aren't you a Texan?"

"Yes, but Texans don't ride in the street." My legs must have clamped around poor Deadly like a vise. I mean, there were cars and motorcycles and buses out there, not to mention construction with actual jackhammers in use at one of the town houses along the way.

My own horses—Plum and Spier—would have been on their way to Waco by this time. Waco is a hundred miles from where I live. On their way to Waco without thinking twice.

Sellers tried to talk to me, but I was way too petrified to pay much attention. I kept waiting for the horses to explode, but both of them, big old Lars and Deadly, were unmoved. Still, even if the racket and the vehicular near misses didn't bother them, they could still slip on the asphalt, couldn't they?

I voiced this fear and was told it was unlikely. "We shoe 'em with borium," Sellers said, "and there's a rubber pad that goes on first, kind of like a shock absorber." Claremont, he went on to say, had its own blacksmith who worked on the premises.

I almost said, *I know*, but caught myself. "How much farther is it?" I asked.

"It's three blocks."

"Three blocks! Are you telling me that we are going to ride these horses through city traffic for three whole blocks?"

"That's right." He named the streets we had to cross, although his voice was practically lost in the city din. They were Amsterdam, Columbus, and Central Park West.

Crossing Amsterdam, our trusty mounts threaded their way through a squealing mob of skateboarding youths.

On Columbus, a motorcyclist slalomed first around Lars and then around Deadly. Neither horse so much as batted an eye.

By the time we came to Central Park West—or CPW, as Sellers called it—I was able to take a breath. I was so invigorated by the dangers I had passed that I almost forgot Sellers was the enemy. "Phew," I called out to him. "Nobody back home will believe I ever did this."

"Look out!" Sellers shouted.

Deadly lurched to a stop just as an ear-piercing horn went off.

I had been looking in Sellers's direction while talking and had very nearly stepped out in front of a truck carrying cabbages. The driver shouted something in a foreign tongue at me and shook his fist as he roared past us.

I was about to tell Sellers that I'd changed my mind about riding when I saw the park ahead through the various lanes of traffic.

The bridle path in Central Park is fabulous—maybe fifteen feet wide, with good feathery footing. There's no cactus to step on, no mesquite to grab at your ear or your shoulder or your clothes. There are no fire ants falling out of trees, no rattlesnakes lying in wait. In short, it beat Texas terrain by a long shot.

"We can trot through here," Sellers called, but before I could even answer, he was doing it. His horse's trot stride was pretty short, so Deadly was able to stay alongside with no difficulty at all. Still, Sellers kept glancing over at me, as if he expected me to be less than fine.

Every time he did, I managed a grin. An idiotically wide one, probably.

"Up for a canter?" he asked.

"Sure."

We blazed past joggers, kids flying kites, nannies wheeling toddlers in strollers, infants in prams. I had taken the lead, and with newfound confidence. Indeed, at this point I wanted to send my horse to the Big Apple for training.

"Who trains these horses?" I asked, swiveling in my saddle so that Sellers would be able to hear me. It was then I noticed that his face was all screwed up and purposeful, as though I'd caught him in the act of thinking menacing thoughts about me.

God, I was getting as paranoid as Flora.

Except that there was no mistaking the way he looked.

"What's the matter?" I asked him, deciding to be brave.

"I've got gas," he said.

A likely story. But very clever on his part, right? Because I wasn't exactly going to demand proof.

"You're from Texas, right?" he went on. "So you probably eat a lot of Mexican food."

"Right."

"Those black beans," he said. "That's what did it. I had a plate of those black beans last night and—"

"All right, that's very clever on your part," I interrupted, slowing my horse to a trot and allowing him to do the same. We trotted side by side, posting. He and Lars dwarfed poor Deadly and me. Still, I thought a head-on approach might work. "But don't think I don't know what's going on here," I said, "because I do. Flora told me."

I saw his eyes widen and his mouth drop open. Then he turned in the saddle and reached down toward me. Right there in broad daylight!

I leaned forward and clucked to Deadly and he responded by shooting forward into a canter again. I pressed my legs against him and he went faster right away, as if delighted to show me his stuff. He probably hadn't galloped in a while, because he took time out for a gleeful little buck.

I looked behind and saw Sellers urging Lars forward. Great. Lars's stride could max out at twice the length of ours. Did I expect to outrun him?

"Watch where you're going," Sellers called. "Low bridge up ahead."

And sure enough. Just ahead loomed a low stone arch—the entrance to a tunnel. I saw movement in the darkness there and could hear rap music from within the tunnel's depths. We would be mugged. But that was preferable to being caught by Sellers and throttled. Plus . . .

Yes! The bridge was so low that Sellers would never be able, on a horse as tall as Lars, to duck sufficiently to enter the tunnel. If he tried, he'd end up being smashed, probably looking like a very realistic mural on the tunnel's ceiling. Ha! Think Sistine Chapel here. So I galloped into the tunnel and immediately reined to a walk.

Sellers figured out the spatial relationship between himself and the tunnel a little too late. I heard him curse as he tried to swerve at the last minute, and I heard a grunt and a thud and a lot of noises that suggested that he and Lars had parted company.

Sure enough, I heard Lars's galloping hoofbeats receding.

Horses are herd animals. Thus, when a horse is galloping away, the one who is standing generally wants to follow suit. Deadly was no exception. He bolted forward, and when I halted him again, he tried to rear.

Looking at the stone ceiling of the tunnel, I couldn't have this happen. I leaned forward, pressing all my weight on his neck. Deadly stood and shook all over, as if he was weighing his options.

Meanwhile, the rap music surrounded us and about seven would-be muggers came up and said things like, "Hiho, Silver!" and "Ride 'em, ace!"

I don't know who was more scared, Deadly or me. Meanwhile, I hadn't heard a peep from Sellers. Not even a moan. I imagined him sneaking up on us, pushing the muggers aside, and catching hold of my leg.

One of the kids reached out toward Deadly—maybe even to pet him, for all that I knew—but it pushed the horse over the edge. He whinnied and whirled and lunged in the direction that his stablemate had run, and I—still pondering the question of clearance—let him.

I say let him as though I were still in charge. The truth is that when Deadly whirled, though I'd somehow managed to stay on board, I wasn't where I ought to have been. I was hanging way to the left, one leg across the saddle, kind of like this was the Pony Express and I was a mere sack of mail.

And Deadly, meanwhile, was not just galloping, but *careening* after Lars. I guess my weight off to the side like that really threatened his balance. But anyway, he was running back the way we'd come. Another five minutes and we'd be in heavy traffic.

I doubted that the terrified Lars, without a rider to guide him, would stop and look both ways before crossing.

But I had problems of my own.

Still, if you ride, you know that regaining my seat was not entirely out of the question. I still had one stirrup. And off on the left side, Deadly and I were making eye contact.

I could see the poor animal's consternation.

You may think I'm venturing into Disneyland here, but I tell you, this is true. Deadly was saying, *Oh-oh, I shouldn't be doing this.*

And I, with my eye, was saying, *Stop doing this!*

And Deadly was saying, *Oh God, oh God, what should I do?*

Meanwhile, though, I managed to wiggle back into the saddle and even find my other stirrup. Thus—and this wasn't easy—I was able to give him a firm clue.

You will whoa, and right this minute, I said with my voice and my hand and my seat, sitting upright and wedging him between my hip and my hand.

And Deadly said, *Yes'm*, and stopped dead.

Even I was impressed. "Good boy," I said, patting his sopping-wet neck.

I have to be honest and admit that my first instinct was to ride toward Claremont and look for Lars. It isn't that I prefer people to horses, or that I preferred Lars to Sellers. It's just that in my experience, the people are always okay after a fall, but the horse is out there getting into trouble. And what with three city streets to cross, Lars was going to be in honkin' big trouble indeed.

Except that he was probably back at Claremont by now and I couldn't chance getting Deadly rolling again because he might not be as easily stopped next time.

Plus Sellers's silence, following the initial groan that I'd heard, must have meant that he'd taken a pretty big hit.

So despite Deadly's reluctance to go away from the stable and all of his friends, I picked up a canter, heading back toward the spot where Sellers had gone off.

There was a growing crowd at the tunnel entrance and atop the tunnel—on the bridge—an ambulance and a police car with its bubble light awhirl. Already! Cops in New York City don't waste any time.

I pressed forward on Deadly, and the crowd parted for us. I could hear people speculating about what had happened.

"Guy got killed by some damn kids in the tunnel," was one theory.

"Horse trampled a guy," was another.

"This girl here musta trampled him," was a third.

"Yeah, dude, here she is. She the one." This last came from one of the kids who had been in the tunnel. He was laughing like crazy, because he knew I hadn't done a thing.

His friends liked this idea. "Hey, officer," another of his chums yelled. "Ask this white girl here what happened."

Well, in a way he was right. I had gone into the tunnel to thwart Sellers, hadn't I?

"Hey, officer, talk to *her*." The kids were practically chanting it now.

I saw an officer's hat come to attention. Then I saw an officer's hat moving in my direction. And I took the coward's way out.

Which is to say that I dismounted so that I wouldn't be sticking up in the air above the crowd the way you do when you're on horseback, and I tried, as well as a woman leading a horse could, to blend into the throng.

I have to say that my strategy also involved moving in the opposite direction, though at a pace that wouldn't in and of itself attract attention.

Impossible, you say?

I'd have thought so, too, except that when I heard the

siren that had to have been the ambulance moving away
with poor Sellers, I was nearly at Central Park West.

Where, I might add, Lars stood at the curb, patiently
grazing.

CHAPTER 6

New Yorkers are an incredible bunch. I mean, here I am, crossing three busy city streets, leading two horses, one the size of the Goodyear blimp, and nobody even bats an eye.

I ask you.

But I'm wondering what I'm going to say when I get on Claremont turf. "Excuse me, but Sellers, the guy who took me on the trail ride? Well, he's dead, but . . ."

I refused to believe that he *was* dead, though, partly because I'd already heard that ambulances don't waste their sirens on dead people and partly because . . . well, I'm not sure. Because I couldn't believe that people die that way, you know, riding toward a tunnel one minute and smashed against the ground another minute, like *splat!* and they're gone.

And also, if I'm supposed to have trampled poor Sellers, wouldn't the police be looking for me? (I could just see the tabloids now, MAD TRAMPLER ROAMS MAN-HATTAN.)

Everything is always so complicated, I decided as I guided Lars and Deadly to their inner-city home.

* * *

"Hello?" My greeting was absorbed by the thick loam footing of the little indoor school. Still, it was plain there was no one to answer it. I strained to look through the dusty glass window at the office, but the desk seemed abandoned.

What? Were they having a fire drill?

But perhaps they'd all rushed off because they'd heard about what happened to Sellers. I don't mean that they'd run off frolicking, I mean that they were viewing the remains or visiting him in the hospital or whatever. Or maybe it was what Flora called "siesta time."

But anyway, it gave me a chance to go into the office and look for the release I'd signed, the one with my name and the name of the hotel where I was staying. That way nobody would find me and accuse me of whatever they planned to accuse me of—making Sellers fall or trampling him, I guess.

I was innocent of this, of course, but I'd seen enough TV and movies to make me worry a little. I mean, think about *The Fugitive*. So there I'd be, years later, with Tommy Lee Jones hot on my trail . . . hmmm. Doesn't sound half bad when you think about it.

And Tommy Lee Jones rides horses, too.

Ah.

The office, the office, I told myself. But before I could get into the office, I had to deal with Lars and Deadly. Although I hated to leave them with their tack on, I remembered that the horses had come into the manège all tacked up. I therefore tucked the reins behind the put-up stirrup irons and gave first Deadly, then Lars, a little pat on the fanny. Sure enough, Lars went to his ramp and clomped down and Deadly went to his ramp and clomped up. Amazing. And I went to the office and began my search.

I found the clipboard, but the paper I'd signed wasn't on it. Similarly, I found a file of signed releases and mine was not among them. So I shrugged and figured I'd better get back to the hotel.

Back to Flora. I'd tell her, for one thing, that every horse I'd seen—the ones the kids were riding in the lesson and the two who had gone to the park—had full tails.

It was true that I now had plenty of opportunity to examine Claremont's other mounts, but it didn't seem fitting to go off reconnoitering. Not with the police probably arriving at any moment with some embarrassing questions.

I know, I know, you're wondering why I wasn't at least a little shaken by the notion that Sellers was hurt, or worse, maybe even out of the picture for good, right? I don't know what to say. Maybe I was in denial. It's popular—and therefore socially acceptable—to be in denial these days.

Anyway, I came out onto Eighty-ninth Street and looked both ways. There were people lurking about, but they didn't seem to be paying me much mind. I turned and started off in the direction of Broadway.

Well, they say we have a sixth sense and mine kicked in to say that something was wrong. I tried to ignore the feeling, but I couldn't. I was being watched. Maybe even followed.

I turned as quickly as I could, but felt like a fool because there was no one there. Ah, but then I saw him. He was on the balcony of one of the buildings along the street, and he was pretending to water some marigolds, but he couldn't fool me.

Sure enough, as soon as he saw me take note of him, he disappeared inside. Gotcha, I thought, walking on. But within minutes, the feeling was back.

I turned and saw two things simultaneously: one was a black-garbed figure climbing out of a limo into Claremont Riding Academy. The other was a person, too, but he or she ducked into a doorway so quickly that I was unable to confirm the person's gender.

I didn't leap to conclusions. Instead I walked another half block and tried turning again.

And then I was sure.

I was being followed.

My inclination—I mean, wouldn't yours be?—was to call the police. But then I remembered Sellers and my hit-and-run behavior—I mean, I *did* leave the scene. And I decided to keep right on.

So I turned down Broadway before I even thought about direction. And I went into the first little clothing shop I came to.

The salesgirl was reading a magazine called *Strange*. She didn't look up from it, which was fine by me. I browsed through the racks of clothing, one eye turned to the window that looked onto the street.

Everything in the store was—well, kind of brassy. I wondered if Flora did her shopping there. On the other hand, maybe I was just hopelessly out of touch with current fashion.

Lord knows, in my real life—my life at Primrose Farm near Austin, Texas—I hardly ever wear a dress or skirt. And there aren't any fashion mags in the mailbox, either. No. Even though our mailman bends beneath the weight of our mail, it's mostly horse magazines that come: *Horse Play* and *The Chronicle* and *Dressage and CT*. Of course, Jeet gets mail, too, but his is like *Gourmet* and *Fine Dining* and stuff.

But I digress.

I yanked something from the hanger and tried to decide if it was a skirt or a cummerbund. A skirt, I guessed. Then I went for the fishnet hose. I imagined what Flora would say when I turned up dressed almost exactly the same way she dressed and decided, hey, it was the sincerest form of flattery, wasn't it? "I'll wear this stuff," I told the clerk. My fifty dollars just did cover it.

When I went outside, the person who had been tracking me was gone. Maybe he'd had to go to the bathroom, I thought, and I just happened to come out of the store while this was taking place. Maybe it was my lucky day.

Meanwhile, I pressed on toward my hotel.

I was about a block away when I got that feeling again. Sure enough, when I turned, the follower tried to dodge. This time he was slower and I caught a flash of pants leg as he ducked out of view.

Ha!

So instead of going directly to my hotel, I took a side trip. I went to the hotel across the street. I walked through the lobby and got into an elevator and emerged on the fifth floor.

Then I found the staircase and went up to the sixth.

Then I took the elevator to the twelfth.

Then the stairs to the ninth.

Then the elevator back to the lobby.

That would show the guy who was on my tail that I was no dummy. I wasn't going to lead him back to my room and back to Flora.

When I came back onto the sidewalk and crossed the street, I checked the way I felt. I was tail-free, I was sure. I broke into a grin and congratulated myself.

And then the most awful thing that has ever happened to me happened: Flora's body came hurtling down from above me and slammed, with a sound every bit as awful as you can imagine, into the street.

I was stunned.

It all happened in the briefest flash, too. I had a sense of the weight of her passing over me just before the impact. When impact came, it was loud and succulent, a sound I know I'll never erase from my memory.

I'm sure you'd rather that I didn't talk about this, but it's like driving past a horrible wreck. You don't want to look. You don't. But of course you do.

What followed was bedlam. People came from every direction, pushing me out of the way and, mercifully, blocking the sight of poor Flora from my view.

I stepped backward as they gathered, almost as though I were dancing. Then I felt something hard and awkward beneath the sole of my shoe.

I bent to retrieve the object and found myself holding what I recognized as Flora's key chain, the keys affixed to the replica of a snaffle bit, in my hand.

My hand began to tremble as I instinctively looked around to see who might have seen me pick it up.

No one was looking my way.

I squeezed the keys—a gesture of sympathy meant for Flora—before slipping them into my handbag.

All I could think of now was Jeet, how much I needed him. How much I needed the consolation of his arms around me. How much I didn't want to be in a huge strange city without him. How much I didn't want to be in a huge strange city at all.

I'd go to our room and I'd call his publisher. If necessary, I'd call every restaurant they'd planned to send him to. I'd call every restaurant in New York, if need be, in order to find him and be with him.

I pushed my way through the crowd and into the lobby of our own hotel. A throng had gathered there as well. I heard someone say something about a jumper, and that was when I realized that Flora hadn't fallen from the window.

No.

She'd committed suicide.

Oh, God. I wondered then, would I have been able to stop her if I'd known or even suspected she was suicidal?

The door to our room was ajar, which should have made me nervous about stepping inside. Instead, I moved even faster, hitting the door so hard that it slammed back against the wall with a huge, cracking sound as I burst inside.

Jeet was there! I didn't have to search restaurants and publishing firms for him, he was there!

But the relief that I felt at the sight of him quickly dissipated, because of the way he was standing there at the window. Despite my abrupt and dramatic entrance, he hadn't budged from his stance. I went up behind him and grasped his shoulders.

"Jeet?" I said.

He turned to face me, an expression of pain on his face. It dissolved into a kind of gratitude. "Oh, my God, Robin," he breathed. "You're all right!" He squeezed me full-length up against himself and started rocking back and forth with me in his arms. He was crooning, "You're all right, you're all right," as if there were a reason that I wouldn't be.

"You thought that was me?" I asked, my voice sort of muffled because of the way I was smooshed up against him.

He separated himself momentarily and looked at me. "I wasn't sure . . . I was afraid . . . it all happened so fast, it was all over in a fraction of a sec—"

"You saw her jump?"

"No, it was worse than that. It was . . . there was this struggle . . . there were people. . . ." He seemed unsure of how to phrase whatever it was.

"Shhh, shhh," I consoled him. "You don't have to talk about it." Except that alarms were going off inside my head. What was my husband talking about? Hadn't Flora been alone? What had he seen?

But fortunately, he went on. "She was . . . she was fighting with him when I opened the door, and he pushed her . . . I mean, if it was a he, it was so incredibly fast, I—"

"Oh, Jeet," I said, thinking, *Pushed!*

"It was awful," he told me. "It was the worst thing

I've ever seen, and I was just standing there in the doorway, I mean, I was sort of frozen there."

It *is* that way when terrible things are happening right before your eyes. You almost don't believe it. You can't act, can't stop anything, really, because you're reduced by the horror of whatever it is, a spectator.

I, alas, know this from experience. Jeet and I sat woefully on the edge of the bed. Jeet got himself more or less together. "Who was she? Who were *they*?" he asked. "What were they doing here?"

I swallowed hard. I should just keep my mouth shut, I told myself, and let him think they were burglars. "She was that girl I told you about. My new friend. Flora Benavides from the riding stable. And he—well, I don't know who he was. Someone Flora knew, I guess."

My mind was eliminating the deceased Sellers from the list of suspects, but who? The guy who followed me, probably. Except I'd never gotten a clear look at him. "How clearly did you see him?"

"Not very. I mean, maybe I'd know him if I saw him again, but I wasn't really registering anything. You know. It was going on—the struggle—when I opened the door and in fact—" He broke off.

"What?" I said.

"In fact, I have the feeling that my coming in . . . well, distracted the girl. I mean, distracted her enough to enable the murderer to get her off balance."

"No. No," I said automatically. This was dangerous thinking, Jeet feeling as if he were somehow to blame. "You didn't see enough to know that." Hadn't he said as much?

"But I know it," he said. "I know it in the way that

you *do* know things," he insisted. "I was responsible."
He waited a minute and then he went on. "Anyway," he
said, "the girl just sort of turned toward me and the
murderer just pushed her over the sill. Just like that.
Then he—" Jeet paused and frowned. "At least, I think
it was a he, but it all happened so fast. . . . He came toward me and I thought, Oh, God, I'm next, but he
didn't even look at me, just rushed past me and went
out the door. It took seconds. The whole thing. Just seconds."

Just then someone cleared his throat and Jeet and I
looked up. A policeman was standing in the hallway
just outside the open hotel-room door.

Twenty minutes later there were two men in suits in
the room as well. They talked to each other loudly,
pointedly, wanting us to overhear. The gist of it was that
Jeet had admitted that he was responsible for Flora's
death and that said admission made their jobs a helluva
lot easier, yessirree.

"That wasn't what Jeet meant," I said, glaring at each
of them in turn.

"Well, maybe you can tell us what you meant," the
first man—both the guys in suits were detectives—said
to Jeet.

"What he meant," I began. But they weren't, they interrupted to tell me, interested in talking to me.

The scenario they came up with was absurd. They
thought Flora was a hooker, and that Jeet had shoved
her out of the window when I, his wife, unexpectedly
came back to the room.

"That's hogwash," I offered, standing up to make my

point. "I was in the *street* when Flora . . . when she . . ."
Oy!—Had I made a crucial error when I'd called the
victim by name?

But that wasn't the part the detective glommed onto.
"What were you doing in the street?" he wanted to
know. Then he eyed me up and down, taking in my
wisp of a skirt, my fishnet hose. "Never mind," he said,
"I think I know."

"How dare you!" I said, sounding like a Victorian
maiden. "I was on my way back from the *hotel* across
the street and—"

Detective number one and detective number two exchanged knowing—maybe even amused—glances.

"Wait just one minute!" I said, on the verge of either
hollering or sputtering or both.

"I'll take care of this," Jeet said, in that calm, assured
way that he has. He began explaining that I'd been ill
that morning and that he'd tried to call, and when I
hadn't answered, he'd become worried. So he'd put the
culinary goodies that awaited him on hold and come
trundling back here, etc., etc. . . .

I was lulled by my husband's voice, thinking that,
once again, he'd made everything all right. I can't tell
you how many times he's been able to quell my anxiety,
even my hysteria, just by talking. This time, though, he
only managed to put my panic on hold.

Because both detectives listened until Jeet was done.

"Nice try," one of them said.

Then the other one fished something out of his suit
pocket and began to read: "You have the right to remain
silent. You have the right . . ."

After he'd tucked the little plastic card back into his

pocket, he stared right at Jeet and declared that he was arresting him for the murder of a woman yet to be identified.

I thought I saw a fleeting flash of fear in Jeet's eye. But then he actually laughed. It wasn't a hearty laugh, of course, but still, it was terribly terribly brave, don't you think? And then he went on with a list of stuff I ought to do, as if he were going out of town for the day or something.

"Robin," he said, picking up his melton jacket and easing into it. "Call Browning at the paper, okay? I'm not sure I'll need him, but I think he ought to know what's going on."

"Browning?" I was dumbfounded.

"In Legal," Jeet said.

"Oh."

"And otherwise," he said, "just sit tight."

"Sit tight?"

"This can't possibly take very long."

"You don't want me to come with you?" I asked him.

"No," he said. "Because Browning will probably be hard to get. The whole thing might be over before you manage to get hold of him."

I saw the two detectives smirk at Jeet's remark.

"That's right, it will be," I affirmed, as pointedly as I could.

"All right," the detective said. "You've been Mirandized. Let's get going."

And we went through it again, kind of like instant replay:

"Robin," Jeet said, looking at me as if he thought his

eyes could cement me down, "call Legal and do *absolutely nothing else*. Promise me."

I stared back at him and felt my lips move, glub-glub, guppylike. I think I was shaking my head yes, as in okay, but I'm not sure. It isn't every day you see your husband hauled away in handcuffs.

And that's what they did, closed these shiny handcuffs that looked like toys around Jeet's wrists, although they had his hands in front of his body and not in the back the way they do on television.

I started out the door behind them, and Jeet turned around and gave me that stare again. He repeated, "Robin. Call Legal. And do absolutely nothing else." I began to think it was a secret code of some kind, a message he wanted to relay even now, daringly, in the presence of the police.

Either that or he meant exactly what he was saying. God, I would make a terrible spy.

I tried taking his advice literally. I stayed there in the room and didn't even look outside to watch them loading Jeet into, I assume, a patrol car. I sat on the bed with my knees up and my arms wrapped around them and I thought about—Jeez!—about the way I loved him.

When I think about love, I always see it from above. There are these concentric valentine-shaped hearts, with various people and—okay, okay, I admit it—horses and dogs and cats and even inanimate objects, *things*, positioned here and there. Some are closer to the center, and some are farther out. It's a sort of combination of Dante and a Parker Brothers game board.

But the point is, Jeet is the only one smack in the middle, the only one who has ever made it into my heart of hearts. He's not even in it, he *is* it, the whole innermost heart space solid with loving him.

Because I do. I love Jeet in a subatomic kind of way, through and through, including—but at the same time way beyond—romance and admiration and respect and whatever else there is. It's like dog love, in that it's no-matter-what.

So, this being the case, I should have listened to him, right? Except that I couldn't, even though I meant to.

I forced myself first to do what Jeet had said to, and put in a call to Browning in the Legal Department at the *Austin Daily Progress* back home. And Jeet was right, no one had the slightest idea when Browning would be back. I said it was an emergency and I left my name and number, and then I wondered just what else I ought to do.

It ticked me off that the police hadn't been the slightest bit interested in asking Jeet his side of the story. Oh, no. They didn't even get to hear about the guy Jeet had surprised pushing Flora to her death. Oh, probably they'd ask when they got to headquarters or something, but basically, as far as they were concerned, Jeet had done the deed.

It *was* like *The Fugitive*. Except that I was on the outside. I could act in Jeet's behalf. I could solve Flora's murder and find the equivalent of the one-armed man. It was a cinch that the police weren't going to even try. And Browning, he was back in Austin.

On the other hand, maybe whoever it was had come to the room for me! For me! I'd been followed, hadn't I? And I'd dodged my follower, enabling him to come here thinking he was hot on my trail. He'd found Flora instead, and . . .

But why?

And what about my promise? To do absolutely nothing, I mean.

I tried to be logical, tried to consider even remote possibilities. The worst was that this had been a random act of violence. That would mean that Jeet was shoulder-deep in trouble. Because then there would be nothing to solve, no clues that could lead logically anywhere. Just one stranger in a city full of strangers, one crazy who had committed a crazy act.

But no.

Flora had been terrified. She'd been terrified of someone—though the someone was Sellers, probably. And Sellers must have had an accomplice. The accomplice had to have done Flora in.

And it had to have something to do with whatever it was about the tails that Flora had inadvertently seen.

But what? Some rare breed of horse, the Manx? Or, hey, a disease whose primary symptom is that the tail hairs fall out, a disease that Sellers was trying to pretend didn't exist. Sure.

Except that even if there were something that would explain why horses were tailless, the fact was, they weren't. They'd had tails, at least the ones that I'd seen.

* * *

But there was my promise to Jeet. My pledge to sit tight and do absolutely nothing beyond the call to Legal. Then there was a knock on the door.

Fate.

But first fear.

Suppose the police had finally tracked me down about my involvement in the Sellers thing? Or worse. Suppose this was Flora's killer returning to kill me?

I swallowed hard. Then I eased the door open and found myself face-to-face with an obviously troubled weasel of a man.

He introduced himself as the interim manager of the hotel. And he told me, with apologies as profuse as the beads of sweat upon his brow, that I had until three that afternoon to surrender the room that Jeet and I had been renting.

"We have two more days!" I shrieked.

"I'm sure you realize . . ." he began, his voice but a hint above a whisper.

"But—"

"And anyway, the management always reserves the right—"

"But . . ."

What it boiled down to in the end was that being arrested for murder, even in New York City, did not make you particularly welcome as a guest. In fact, you moved from Marginal into Downright Undesirable as a result. None of my threats—well, actually, calling the Better Business Bureau was the only one I made—or my pleas made a dent.

"Do I get a phone call?" I asked, thinking that Jeet's agent probably would help.

"Is it local?" the manager wanted to know.

Except that I got their answering machine. You know how that is. I left a message saying who I was and that I needed help and would call back. I mean, you don't exactly want to commit to Memorex the information that your husband has been arrested for murder, now do you? Also, maybe I should be glad they weren't there. I mean, do agents really want potential felons for clients? I mean, writing cookbooks?

Back in Texas, I would have had my own support system. My best friend, Lola, to name one person in it. But maybe I could talk Lo into flying up to . . .

To what? Hold my hand? Sure, she'd come, but really, what could she do?

So I had to face it: I was on my own.

I hadn't thought to ask Jeet for his wallet when the police had taken him away, so I was also penniless.

And homeless, besides.

Except that, even as the concept of sleeping in a doorway covered by a flattened-out cardboard box came to mind, I was closing my fingers around Flora Benavides's keys.

CHAPTER 7

I don't know. I seem like a nice normal person. I mean, I look in the mirror and that's what looks back at me, a very normal not-bad-looking thirty-six-year-old housewife. Round face, blunt-cut brown hair about two inches shy of my shoulders, big round brown eyes.

Which is why, when I said to the policeman on the corner, "Excuse me, but my husband has been arrested and I'd like to get him out on bail," he looked astonished.

"I'm serious," I told him.

"Arrested for what?"

"For, uh, murder."

He narrowed his eyes, taking my measure. And he decided—I could see—that I was crazy as a loon. Nonetheless he talked to me anyway, probably in the event I decided to sue the NYPD.

"So what's the problem?" he asked.

"I need to know how much the bail is and I don't know how to find out. I don't even know where the detectives took him."

"When did this happen?"

"About twenty minutes ago."

"He's probably not in the system yet."

I nodded. Tried to figure out what he meant. Then, when I couldn't, I asked, "Meaning what?"

"Meaning the computer probably doesn't have him logged in. So, being as you don't know, you won't be able to find him until it does. Until he's logged in, that is."

Oh, Jeet! Lost in the system! He could end up staying lost, too. I'm sure things like that have happened. Probably there were legions of men—maybe women, too—who were lost in the system. Right there on the street, standing next to this cop, I could see myself on *Oprah* describing Jeet's travail, and my own.

"So, uh," the cop added.

"So, uh." I accepted and walked on. And where did I think I was going to get the money to bail Jeet out anyway? I had, thanks to my shopping foray, zip in the way of cash, not counting some change. That, and Jeet's plastic.

I looked down at the skirt I was wearing. Would the store—assuming I could find the store—take it back? I mean, I still had my unitard in the mammoth carpetbag purse I carried, so it wasn't as though I'd have to Godiva my way through the streets. I sure wasn't going to give that worm at the hotel the satisfaction of going back and begging for my suitcase, which of course I hadn't even thought about until now. It's hard to think efficiently when you're being evicted.

As I was thinking this I watched a frustrated tourist—even I could spot them by now—losing a quarter in a pay phone. Which is when I, Robin Vaughan, against my will, knew I was going to have to get illegal.

I spied a clothing store and went inside and emerged with a coat hanger. It cost me all I had left in cash, which turned out to be eighty-nine cents. I viewed it as an investment—you know, spending money to make money.

You remember what the operator told me after I, like the tourist I'd just seen, had lost major amounts of change in the pay phone, don't you? That kids will stuff a plastic bag up into the return slot so that coins will fall and lodge there instead of falling into the little cup where you're supposed to retrieve the money you put in. Well, I thought, I could use some money right now, so . . .

I mean, a girl's got to eat.

What an amazing place New York is. I mean, there I am, a normal-looking thirty-six-year-old housewife, in broad daylight, Roto-Rootering the pay phones on every block, and nobody bats an eye.

Amazing.

I dumped my take out on Flora Benavides's narrow bed. I had gone from penniless and homeless to having more than fifty dollars to play with. In quarters.

Jackpot, I thought.

Meanwhile I called Browning at the *Austin Daily Progress* yet again and told him—or rather his voice mail—to leave a message for me at Flora's building in her name. It was the best I could do.

This time I went a wee farther out on the limb, though, and mentioned that a speedy return call would be a good thing because Jeet was in trouble.

Anyway, now I had to approach the desk.

Behind it was a girl with blue hair—or a strip of hair, at least—and a ring through her eyebrow. I swear. And her hair wasn't blue the way old ladies' hair is blue, but bright blue, electric blue.

"I'm Flora Benavides's friend," I said.

Blue hair looked up. Her eyes were made up like Tammy Faye Bakker's, which is to say that I'm surprised she could lift her lids for all the mascara she'd applied. She probably had stronger lids than I had abs.

"Oh," she said, smiling and actually looking cute. "Cool!" she allowed. "Tell Flora hello."

I wish I could, I thought.

Unbidden, an image of Flora as I'd last seen her came to me. Oh, God. I almost lost it remembering how purple she had been, and how hideously mushy and misshapen. I wanted to scream. I lowered my eyes so she couldn't see them fill.

Then she knocked me for a loop. "So this Jeet is in trouble, huh."

I stared at her. What was she, like Wanda, a practicing psychic?

She gestured at the telephones on the nearby landing. "Hard not to hear," she explained.

My first thought was, Oh, no! That meant I wouldn't be able to make any calls about Jeet without her finding out that he'd been arrested for murder. And as soon as she found out, I'd be back on the street. Unless . . .

"He was arrested," I said.

"Cool!" she answered.

"For murder."

"Oh, *super* cool!" Those eyelids of hers were getting a real workout today.

"So, I'll be, like, calling to find out where they took him."

"Riker's, I'll bet."

"Riker's?"

"Riker's Island. That's where everyone gets arraigned."

"What's your name?" I asked her. I like thank-yous to be personal.

"Tubular," she said.

"Your first name," I clarified.

"Tubular," she told me. "And anyway, I only have one. One name, that is."

We looked at each other for a beat. Then I said, "Well thank you, Tubular. Really."

Have you ever called one of these huge bureaucratic places like Riker's Island and tried to get information? You get a recording (in English and Spanish). Inmate-and-bail information, press one. Unless you're fast enough or you aren't used to thinking of the man you married as an inmate. Then you wait for the operator, who turns out to be a man with absolutely the deepest voice you've ever heard. And he tells you that your husband was probably taken to a precinct, and which one depends on where he was arrested.

So I was back at the desk. "Tubular," I asked, "why did you think that Jeet would be taken to Riker's?"

"Why?"

"Why."

"Because that's where they take them on *Cagney and Lacey*," she said.

I squint at her. "*Cagney and Lacey*," I say, "was before your time."

"It's in reruns," she explains.

I am hungry. My stomach churns. I think of Jeet in the bowels of the New York Department of Correction eating prison food. Prison food! My husband, the gourmet!

And I debate. Solving Flora's murder wins out over trying to locate Jeet. It's solving Flora's murder that will free Jeet, after all.

So the minute it gets dark, I will go down the flight of stairs and onto Broadway knowing that that's what I've gotta do.

But meanwhile, I have to kill time in Flora's apartment lest I be tempted to spend my meager store of coins.

Flora's apartment. I began by looking at her clothes. She had been really tiny, and her clothes, of course, reflected this. All of the skirts, for instance, were of the itty-bitty variety. Some of them, however, were made of stretchy fabrics. Dresses were like that, too.

I wiggled into the stretchiest one of these and stood in front of the full-length mirror.

It wasn't a pretty sight.

I imagined Flora going on a job interview dressed like this. Then I imagined myself doing the same. I got into it, pretending to be Lily Tomlin, picking up an imaginary telephone the way she used to when she played that person from the phone company—was it

Ernestine? Except that I didn't work for the phone company, I worked for a law firm.

The outfit inspired me. I cooed the name of the firm: "Shameless and Wanton," I said. Then I added, "An equal opportunity employer."

Ha. If I had to get a job up here, I'd put that down as my last employer. That way, if they got it, they would think I was superclever and want to hire me. And if they didn't, well, they'd at least think I had an employment history—which, of course, if you know me, you know I don't.

I'm a housewife. A vampire. A leech. I live off Jeet. Oh, don't get all politically correct on me, because I cook, I clean, I do all the leather: saddles, bridles, riding boots, and my husband's shoes and briefcase. I fix plumbing, wiring, sink fence posts, mend wire. I am not the useless sycophant I seem.

Still, if Jeet goes up the river, I *will* need a job.

Unless I can make a career of robbing pay phones.

But I'm getting ahead of myself.

I continued with Flora's wardrobe, moving on to the contents of a cardboard box on the floor.

Oh. A thousand and one nighties. I held these up. Apparently, visibility and access were uppermost in Flora's mind.

But why? She was a stable girl.

My own wardrobe consists, in the main, of breeches and jeans and torn, grass- and slobber-stained T-shirts.

I faced the awful conclusion: maybe Flora *was* a hooker on the side.

Just then there was a knock on the door. Was it a john? And if so, what?

I opened the door. It was Tubular. She was carrying a stack of magazines. "You forgot these," she said.

I took them from her. I guess I looked puzzled.

"It's Flora's mail," she said. Then she said she couldn't stay because she was on the desk.

"This is Flora's mail?" I said. This was a nine-inch stack of magazines here. "When's the last time she picked it up?"

"Oh, that's just today's," Tubular told me. "But she gets, like, every fashion mag there is."

Indeed.

I hadn't even heard of most of them, though the old standbys—*Vogue*, *Harper's Bazaar*, *Elle*—were there, too.

I set them down and then remembered the stack of fashion magazines I'd seen the first time I was here. And sure enough, there they were, in the closet. I pulled them out.

Fashion magazines did not jibe with the Flora I knew. Did not jibe with the clothes in Flora's closet, either. Unless fashion has begun, now, to embrace the chippy look.

I pulled a few of them down. There were paper clips on some of the pages. I opened to them.

The first was a Mia ad—a kind of safari background except that all of the big white hunters had cameras instead of guns. A woman in a Mia suit—with the braid and the big woven buttons—stood in the center.

Guess who the model was? The woman who had made the scene in the Indian restaurant, the one with the black-black hair and the white-white skin.

MIA, the ad said. BECAUSE IT'S YOUR WORLD, TOO.

I started flipping through all of the mags, checking all of the paper-clipped pages. They were Mia ads, all. Various backgrounds, all of some ecological import, with the same woman in the center.

I ran down to the desk. "Tubular," I said, holding up one of the ads. "Do you know who this is?"

"Sure. It's Mia. She's, like, into saving the planet. The animals, anyway."

"Flora was such a big Mia fan," I said. "Do you know why?"

"No. Why?"

"Oh. Well, I don't know. I thought you would."

"No, I don't know," she said.

How come conversations never go this way for Miss Marple? I mean, is it me?

"Did you ever see Flora in a Mia suit?" I tried.

"Flora? What are you, nuts?"

"Did you ever see her dressed up?"

"Well, sure," Tubular said. "Dressed up the way you are." She pointed at my itsy-bitsy teeny-weeny dress.

I swear, I blushed.

"Tubular," I said. "Do you know how Flora made her living?"

"Something about horses," she said. "She rode them or something."

This was going nowhere, I decided. Or everywhere. One or the other, I didn't know which.

"Tubular," I said, "did you ever see Flora with a man?"

"A man." She seemed puzzled.

"Or various men," I clarified.

"Um, I don't think so."

So maybe she wasn't a hooker. But why hadn't Tubular seen her roommate, the one whose jeans I'd worn? And where were those jeans, come to think of it?

"Tubular," I said, realizing that I was actually enjoying saying her name, "what do you think of this dress?" I stood back so she could get the full effect.

"On you? Well, uh . . ."

I went back upstairs and changed into my unitard. I selected a big black top to go with it. And then I sat on the bed and continued looking through the magazines.

None of the clothes inside were quite like Flora's. They were—how had Flora put it? Upper East Side cool. So Flora having all these magazines—and marking all of the Mia ads, of course—was pretty off-the-wall.

Which meant that knowing this might help free Jeet.

Awright! I was getting closer. When I came to an actual article about Mia, I immersed myself in it.

Mia. She sounded way too good to be true. She supported all kinds of animal-rights causes, including the Hooved Animal Humane Society and the Horse Welfare Committee. And she had a reasonably horsey background, too, riding fat ponies bareback in the summertime and taking dude-ranch vacations and such. It wasn't the obsessive kind of horsiness that had overtaken Flora and me, but it was something. It was enough for me to conclude that Mia was a woman who was—in terms of causes, anyway—on the same side.

And she seemed to follow through on her beliefs, stressing, when she talked to the interviewer, that she checked out every soap and cosmetic that came in contact with her skin to make sure there was nothing in the ingredients or even the testing procedures used when creating the product that was in any way abusive to animals of any kind.

The clincher, though, was that she didn't even wear leather shoes or carry a leather handbag. She opted for vinyl, she said, because nothing had to die that way in the name of fashion. Vinyl!

A Mother Teresa of the four-legged, Mia was. Maybe that was the source of Flora's interest in her. Maybe she was a role model for Flora rather than the clue I'd thought I'd just stumbled upon.

I stared long and hard into the full-page Mia head shot. She had pale clear skin and an oval face and eyes as black as sloe, very moist and luminous. Her black hair in this shot wasn't boy-short. Instead, it was parted in the middle and brought straight back into a bun at the nape of her neck, like a flamenco dancer's. She was simplicity personified, and yet I couldn't quite picture her with the halo that ought to be drawn around her head. In fact, she reminded me of someone, though a someone that I couldn't place. I tried and tried to think of who, but couldn't.

I closed the magazines and restacked them where they'd been. Who? Who?

Then a fortunate distraction, because you know how crazy something like that can make you: another knock on the door. Tubular.

"Enter!" I shouted, my back to the door.

A big mistake.

It's odd, isn't it, how many of our animal instincts survive. Because, without turning around, I knew that the person who was standing in the doorway wasn't Tubular at all.

And okay, you can talk about air displacement and body heat and cite whatever physical law would cover this, but the fact is, without even wondering or thinking about it, I knew someone big was there.

Slowly I turned.

"You!" I said, pointing at him.

Sellers.

"My God!" I followed up. And sank in a bewildered heap back onto the edge of Flora's bed.

He came in and shut the door. "Nice going," he said. "I had you figured for a screamer."

I don't know why I hadn't screamed. Maybe I'd given up. Or maybe in some hopeful part of me I'd thought, If he's alive and unhurt, Flora can be alive and unhurt, too. I don't know.

"What are you doing here?" I asked.

"I've got to talk to you about Flora," he said. "I've got to talk to you about this whole thing. See, in a sense, she was my partner," he explained.

"Right," I said.

"Look, do you want to hear the story or not?"

"Fine," I said. "Let's hear the story."

"Look," he said, "this room is kind of small for me. Let's go someplace and talk."

To say the room was small was understatement. I had been surprised to see that he was able to pass through the frame of the door. I mean, if you turned him into liquid, he'd probably fill the dimensions of the room nearly to the top.

"So can we?" he asked.

"Sure," I said.

He and I stared at each other. The problem of my leaving first had occurred to both of us. Don't ask me how I knew that, but I did, and it was a stupid thing to think about, under the circumstances. But face it, we're all creatures of custom and custom has it that the woman exits before the man.

Except that it wasn't going to be possible. In fact, *turning* to exit, for Sellers, wasn't going to be possible either.

He backed out of the room. I pressed forward and left, too—as though we were dancing. The temperature in the hall seemed twenty degrees cooler than it was inside Flora's room.

"Flora's dead," I said.

"I know."

"I thought *you* were dead," I said. "Or seriously hurt."

"I know."

We moved past the reception desk.

"Is there a Cure concert tonight?" Tubular asked.

"Huh?"

"She means your outfit," Sellers explained. "The Cure is a rock group and it is customary to wear all black when one goes to see them."

"Standard fat girl's outfit," I explained.

"Who are they?" Tubular wondered.

Sellers yanked my arm before I could tell her that wasn't the name of a band, and somewhat gratefully, I followed him. Then we were down the stairs and outside on the street.

Sellers was huffing so much that I wondered how

he'd gotten *up* the stairs. He must have started hours earlier.

"Where do you want to go?" I asked him.

"I don't care," he said. "One of those coffee places on Broadway."

"Okay," I said. We could walk until we came upon one. I turned to the right, but he grabbed my arm.

"You don't want to go that way," he said. "Come on."

New York is the oddest place. I mean, there can be a really pricey and relatively safe neighborhood right next to one that's like a combat zone. And the thing is, New York people know where all these little crime pockets are, I mean, as though there's a feature on them on the nightly news right between the sports and the weather. They—meaning New Yorkers—will say, "Amsterdam is okay up to around *X*, but then switch over to Broadway, know what I mean?" It's a kind of insider knowledge that I always envy. They have insider language, too, like knowing that Houston Street is pronounced How-ston here. Or that—I think it was Flora who told me this—people from New Jersey are the B&T crowd, meaning "bridge and tunnel."

Or maybe I'm just easily impressed.

But anyway, by the time I'd mused about all of this, we'd come to a coffee place that Sellers deemed acceptable. We went in. Both of us stared at the bentwood chairs. They sure weren't going to hold the likes of Sellers.

"No, come," a heavily accented voice said. An old man in a spiffy blue-striped apron came around the counter. He was wheeling an oversized metal chair, one that looked as though it could hold an elephant.

Or Sellers.

We sat and ordered espresso. He ordered two chocolate croissants. I always thought that if a doctor examined me and said, "You have a month to live," I would make the best of it. I'd start with all-you-can-eat chocolate croissants. It was going to be hard to watch something that yummy being consumed across the table from me without breaking down and having one—or two—myself.

I looked away when the man in the apron placed the luscious little crescents, all crisp and flaky, and flecked with an oozy cocoa brown, in front of us. Us. One for me, one for Sellers. And here I'd thought he'd ordered them both for himself.

"I don't want one," I said, pushing my plate across to him. *Liar, liar,* my stomach said.

He didn't protest. He pulled the plate around and lined it up behind the first.

"Did the horse get back okay?" he asked.

"Lars? Yeah."

"I figured he would."

"I was dazed," he said. "I remember an ambulance and a wall and, I don't know. No kidding. I couldn't think straight until the ambulance dropped me off."

Good. Then he didn't hold me responsible for ducking into the tunnel where he couldn't possibly follow.

But he had been reaching toward me when I decided to do it. He had been menacing. For some reason, I didn't feel any of that now. But it's hard to be afraid of someone whose face and hands are smeared with chocolate.

"Those kids tried to tell the police that I trampled you," I said, an attempt at bonhomie.

"What kids?"

I tried to remember what the kid who first yelled had looked like. "The kid who started it was young. Black. Well, sort of mocha brown, like that!" I pointed at a particularly yummy-looking iced pastry in the glass display case.

"Is description your specialty?" Sellers asked.

"Well, let me think. He had a goatee, and he wore this cap, knitted, that was black and green and red."

"Anything else?"

"An earring. He had a miniature chain saw hanging off his ear."

"Honey, this is New York City. Half the kids on the street look like that. Except that he obviously wasn't really a kid because kids don't have beards."

"He was a boy," I said stiffly. "Maybe seventeen. But I didn't think you could say 'boy' anymore without getting into trouble."

Sellers laughed.

"How do you know that Flora is dead?" I asked him. Clearly she hadn't been identified. If she had, Tubular would have known, and maybe the police would have come to her apartment.

"I was there," he said. "Right behind you. I was following you."

"Aha!" I said. "I knew it." But wait! The person I'd seen hadn't been fat. Plus the ambulance had taken Sellers away, hadn't it? I voiced these concerns.

"The ambulance dropped me at the hospital," he said, "but I didn't go in. I went right back to the stable. I got there just when you were leaving, so I followed."

"And did I go right to my hotel?" I tested.

He laughed. "You went shopping. And then you went to the hotel across the street from yours and ..." He went on to accurately relay all the floor hopping I'd done.

He leaned forward. "You aren't afraid of me," he said. "If you thought I was some kind of master criminal, wouldn't you be? So think about it. How come you're not afraid?"

"I don't know. Because I could outrun you if I had to. I don't know."

"What if I had a weapon?"

"But you don't. Or you would have used it by now."

"Are you sure that's it?" he asked.

"No. I don't know." Maybe I'm just tired, I thought. Beaten down by all that's happened.

"Well, there's something you should know," he said. And then he stopped. He looked past me to the plate-glass window that fronted the street. Something had caught his eye. He stood up and the metal chair flew backward, crashed into the refrigerated display case.

I turned to see if anything had broken or if the proprietor was mad.

"Jesus," Sellers said, "those three thugs again." He looked at me. "I've seen them before. I think it's you they're after."

"Thugs?" I said, swiveling.

And in the little stretch of time that all that took, Sellers was out the door and gone, and I had to shell out every piece of change I had on me to pay for what we'd eaten and drunk.

I didn't make it. The proprietor looked as though his eyes were about to cross as I dug in every pocket of my handbag as well as every pocket in the skirt and top I wore. I was going to have to go to the pay phones again. Or else back to Flora's to get the rest of my quarters. Because I was sixty-two cents short.

"You come back and pay me," he said. He was so downcast, I could tell he didn't think I would.

"I will," I told him. "Thanks."

I looked outside. No Sellers. No thugs. A woman was walking a dalmatian puppy, trying to manage the pup as it foraged about in the gutter along with a long-handled pooper-scooper that she carried.

Then it hit me about Mia, who it was she'd made me think of: Cruella De Vil. Cruella De Vil in *One Hundred and One Dalmatians*.

It was a scarier thought than you'd think—far scarier than it should have been.

CHAPTER 8

I buzzed my way into Flora's and loaded my purse with quarters.

Oh, God. Oh, God. Jeet in prison, and Flora dead, and me being chased through the streets of New York by thugs. Oh, God.

But after this brief lament, I began to look around for a way out. I would go downstairs, outside, and find a cop, I thought, and ask for protection.

I trundled down the stairs and out the door.

Once outside, though, I felt really threatened and vulnerable. And there wasn't a cop in sight.

I had to keep moving, I decided. I couldn't, even though I had all that change that I got from the telephones in my pocket now, chance waiting for a bus or stopping to hail a cab.

Of course, if my stride *coincided* with the appearance of a bus at a stop or a cab at the curb, I'd be home free.

As it was, however, I could only try to stay ahead of them. Assuming Sellers hadn't lied when he spied them.

I looked over my shoulder. Nope. Because there they were.

Three of them. Strapping, you would have to say, which means that even though they were young, they were bigger than I was. Much bigger. And probably armed.

I tried not to think of the click of a switchblade opening. Not that I'd ever heard such a click before, but I'd seen movies. So I was prepared to hear it, every nerve in my body tensed and ready, waiting for it. *Click!*

I poured on the speed, not running, because I knew that my lungs wouldn't take it, but walking as fast as I could. In New York, this wasn't even mildly out of place. Everyone hustled in New York.

Including the three young men.

Oy.

It was then that I saw some burly deliverymen propping open a doorway between a video store and a deli. I glanced up to see where that doorway might lead. It led to a beauty shop called Afrique.

I dashed for it, pushed past the men, and pounded up the stairs and practically fell inside. A pretty black woman with red hair seemed amused by my entrance. "Hey," she said.

"Hey," I answered. I have always been quick to assume the local patois.

"You here for some braids, right?" she asked.

"Uh, yes," I said.

"Akwana!" she hollered. "Bring that book with the braids out." Then she turned back to me. "You should have told me you were Caucasian. You sure didn't sound Caucasian. Anyway, you look through this, you hear, and see how long you want your braids to be."

How long. I understood making hair shorter, but the concept of lengthening one's hair was new to me.

"Okay," I said, taking a magazine from Akwana's hand.

I walked over to the window and glanced down. The menacing trio was down there, waiting. Here I thought I'd been so smart, but in fact, by coming to Afrique, I'd run into the urban equivalent of a blind canyon.

"Could I use your phone?" I asked. I'd have the police pick them up.

"Phone ain't working," the redhead said. "Should be back on soon, though, if the phone company told us the truth."

Great.

"Okay," I said, "so go ahead and do my hair." I reached into my pocket to make sure Jeet's credit card was still in there. "How long will it take?"

"You in a hurry?" the redhead asked. " 'Cause you can't do this in a hurry. This takes as long as it takes."

I thought about the three young men outside. "Cool," I said.

Akwana wet my hair and poured a conditioner on it. Then she plopped a shower cap on my head and handed me a big stack of magazines. The redhead seemed to have gone.

Akwana saw me looking for her. "Dorrance is the owner," she explained. "She's gone out to buy your hair."

Buy my hair. "Oh," I said.

And sure enough, Dorrance came back in with—yes!—a band of hair that approximated my own chestnut shade. Each strand was about a foot long. "We gonna braid this in with your own hair," Akwana explained. "You gotta do that with Caucasian hair 'cause it's so skimpy, dig?"

I nodded.

"You gotta keep your head still," Dorrance said.

I stopped nodding.

Akwana whipped the shower cap off my head and peered at my scalp. Then she whirled the chair around. "It's better if you don't look until we done," she said. To ensure this, she draped a bed sheet over the mirror so I wouldn't be tempted.

It was around four o'clock when I'd stumbled into Afrique. Now it was six-something. Akwana and Dorrance were both working on me, and my rear end felt as if I'd been on a hundred-mile endurance ride.

But every time I looked outside, there they were, the three guys.

Persistent.

"Girl, what you be looking out that window for?" Akwana wanted to know.

I was afraid I sounded crazy. But I told her. "I'm being followed," I said. "Those three guys down there."

"Those boys?" she said.

"Hmmph," Dorrance, at her side looking down into the street, commented. "Why they following you?"

"I wish I knew."

"Well," Dorrance said, "they got a long wait."

"Which means it takes how long?" I asked.

Now Dorrance told me. "About seven hours," she said.

Seven hours?

Seven hours?

I stood up. "I can't," I said. "I would rather be assaulted in the street than spend seven hours in a beauty shop." I have never even had a permanent. I mean, in my entire life! I tried to explain this. Fruitlessly.

"You sit yourself down," Dorrance commanded. "You can't go out half-done like that. And we bought all this hair."

I sighed deeply, pointedly, and sat.

"Maybe she's hungry," Akwana said. "Maybe we should chip in on a pizza."

My taste buds roused themselves.

"Three of us," Akwana continued. "We could get a medium."

My taste buds segued into a step-aerobics routine.

"I don't know," Dorrance said. "I was thinking Chinese."

"Anything," I said. "I don't care."

I ought to mention that despite their conversation, their fingers never stopped doing whatever it was that they were doing to my hair.

I remembered whining when my mother insisted on rolling my hair for the senior prom. "You have to suffer to be beautiful," my mother said. To her credit, she didn't usually talk this way.

And I answered, "I don't want to be beautiful,"

which has always sort of been my guiding philosophy. Now, here I was, like the mistress of Tara, with two women working away at me.

And it did hurt.

I mean, there are all these sociological inquiries into why women stay in painful situations—I mean physically painful ones—and all these speculations about women and masochism. I say it goes back to simple beauty practices, which prepare us for pain. Which make us think, really, that pain is part of the deal.

I mean, think about it. Plucking our eyebrows. Piercing our ears (or, for the more adventurous, our navels). Having our bikini hairs waxed.

Oh, God. Having our bikini hairs waxed, which I did one time and one time only. You know the scene in *Marathon Man* where Laurence Olivier is about to torture Dustin Hoffman and he takes out a bag of dentistry tools and everybody in the audience spontaneously groans and cringes? Well, for women who have had their bikini hairs waxed, you could do this scene substituting the wax for the dentistry tools and get the same reaction.

And did you ever try using that little tool with the rotating rubber deal that grabs the hair and yanks it? I forget what it's called, Epilady, I think. This is something you pay money for and use at home. When you've been bad. When you've been very very bad.

What was I doing here, being yanked on for hours and hours and hours?

"We should have given her dreads," Akwana said, and she and Dorrance laughed.

"What are dreads?" I asked.

Akwana reached for a magazine.

Dorrance stayed her hand. "Don't go showing her that," she said. "Not now."

Akwana pulled free and handed me the magazine she'd been enjoined not to. I found myself staring at what looked to me like braids gone bad.

"Dreads is forever," Akwana said. "You gotta cut them out. Braids like we doing to you, you can take right out if you want. Dreads is like all matted up and fried."

Probably another seven-hour procedure, I thought. And was any of this—braids included—safe for human hair? I mean, you braid horses for shows, but you have to be sure to take the braids out right away or else their manes break off at the roots. Was that going to happen to me? Oy. I imagined myself virtually bald except for tiny tufts of fuzz here and there on my scalp. But it was that or the guys downstairs. "Wait a minute," I said, feeling the need to stall as well as the need to eat. "Let's get a pizza or some egg rolls or something, like you said, okay? I'm hungry."

Bald. You would have to be gorgeous to pull that off. And while I was okay—I mean, most people said "cute"—I didn't think bald would work for me.

Hmmm. "One of you call the restaurant, please, please, please?" I said. "I want to see if those guys are still down there."

I moved to the window, thinking about horses and braids again.

But horses break their braids off by rubbing them

against things. Trees or the walls of their stall. I wasn't going to do that. So my braids wouldn't break off.

I felt better. Until, that is, I saw the three fellows down there *still* waiting. God. Why didn't they get jobs as sentries or something?

Dorrance picked up the phone. "Still dead," she said.

Akwana must have been hungry. "I don't mind walking," she said. "I'll go get the pizza or the Chinese or whatever you want."

Way to go, Akwana!

Dorrance argued. "I'll go. I'm getting too old for braiding." She waved her hand and clenched and unclenched her fingers. "I practically got arthritis in my bones. So I'll go. You keep working."

We agreed on pizza.

We agreed on pepperoni and peppers and onions.

And then Dorrance was headed out again.

"Watch out for those guys down there," I cautioned her.

"The day guys like that scare me," Dorrance said, "is the day I'll have to move my fine self out of Harlem."

"Is this Harlem?" My eyes were huge. Oh, God. Jeet hadn't mentioned me staying out of Harlem. Harlem was probably like Central Park and the subway all rolled into one.

"This is the West Side. Harlem is where I live. Harlem is where I grew up."

"It's where I live, too," Akwana added. "It starts at Ninety-sixth Street."

Ah. Flora lived in Harlem.

"So, like, you can tell us why these boys is after you," Dorrance said, " 'cause we done heard it all."

I sighed.

"It has something to do with the horses at Claremont Riding Academy," I said. "Only I don't know what. And they killed somebody about it, a friend of mine. Flora. They pushed her out a window. Only the police think my husband did it, and they arrested him."

"You got a man in jail?" Dorrance asked. "Well, honey, why didn't you say so? Let me welcome you to the club."

"Oh, God," I said. Then: "Listen, while you're out there, Dorrance, could you call the police about those guys?"

"I ain't calling no police," she said.

" 'Specially on a brother," Akwana nodded.

"Three brothers," Dorrance said. "Three brothers that, far as I can see, didn't do nothing 'cept stand around waiting."

"They pushed my friend out a window," I said.

Dorrance and Akwana looked at each other the way—well, the way so many people I know have looked at each other over something I've said.

I realized this was futile. Akwana and Dorrance were black. My potential assailants were black. The shop was called Afrique, and that huge outline of Africa, banded in black with its interior a swirl of red and green, wasn't taking up a whole wall for nothing. Ethnically speaking, these women were not on my side.

"Those boys out there never heard of Claremont Riding Academy," Dorrance said.

"You better believe it," Akwana seconded.

It did seem far-fetched. I mean, the boys were as far from tweedy riding types as you can get. But they were definitely after me. And it couldn't be coincidence that they were after me immediately following the murder of Flora Benavides.

"I need pizza," I said. "Let me give you some money."

"When I get back," Dorrance said, and was gone.

Meanwhile, the flying fingers of Akwana kept on. "What's your husband in for?" she asked.

"Murder."

I felt the fingers freeze. Then they started up again and she said, "He do it?"

"No."

"That's what I thought," she said. A longer pause than before. Then: "Is he Caucasian?"

"Yes. Hey, could I see a mirror now?" I asked.

"Naw. You promised, remember?"

"I know, but—"

"Naw. We almost done. You doing real good, real good."

"Yes, but how, exactly, does it look?"

"It looks fine, just fine."

Downstairs, the door slammed open. My heart went boom. But Akwana just laughed. "That's Dorrance telling us that she got too much to carry," she said. Then she hollered, "Be right there," and she finished yanking at my skull and walked off to help Dorrance tote the pizza and drinks up the stairs.

* * *

The luscious smell of cheese and dough and pepperoni filled the room, filled my senses. I was salivating like a dog.

Dorrance laid the pizza box atop a glass display case and opened the lid. Steam rose from the pie inside. "Oh, yum yum," she said.

We gorged ourselves, eating two pieces each. There were two more in the box and I lusted after them, my hunger warring with my desire to more or less be polite. My hands were greasy and, I was sure, my mouth was wreathed in oil and sauce. I didn't care. Dorrance had brought Cokes, too, and I downed mine without even asking if it was diet. I watched glumly as Dorrance ate one of the remaining pieces. Then I watched Akwana to see if there was any hope for me.

"You want that?" she asked me.

"Naw," I said.

At last we were done. I, for one, was glad I was wearing all that Lycra.

Dorrance belched. The three of us laughed.

"What do I owe you?" I asked, reaching down for my purse.

"It comes to about six-fifty apiece."

"What a deal," I said, fishing out a handful of the quarters I had boosted from various telephones around town. I began to count them.

Akwana and Dorrance exchanged those looks again.

"Don't you have bills?" Dorrance asked. I felt as though, if she knew me a little better, she'd have added, "like normal people?"

"Well," I said, "no."

"You aren't planning to pay this shop in quarters, are you?"

"For my hair?"

"For your hair."

"Well, uh, no."

"How are you planning to pay the shop if you don't have no bills?" she asked.

"I have a credit card," I said, "and you have to be quiet while I count." Six-fifty would be twenty-four quarters, wouldn't it?

Dorrance asked, "Why you got all those quarters?"

I sighed. This was rapidly becoming my standard response.

"Why?" she repeated.

"Because I sort of stole them. I needed to. See, when they arrested Jeet—he's my husband—I didn't have any money, but I needed some, so I . . ." And I launched into the story about taking the plastic stuffing out of the telephone coin-return slots and retrieving all the quarters that had lodged there.

Akwana and Dorrance spoke in unison. "Hmmm," they said.

"Hmmm what?" I asked.

They were talking to each other now. "She don't know," Akwana was saying.

"She can't be that dumb," Dorrance was arguing.

"Don't know what?" I asked.

They both turned toward me. Finally Dorrance scrunched down so her face was about four inches away from mine. "Girl," she said, "you are outta your little braided head."

I considered saying something neutral, like, Thank you for sharing, but I didn't have a chance.

Akwana pushed Dorrance away. "I'm telling you, Dorrance, she just didn't know. She's from out of town someplace. And not only that, she's Caucasian."

Dorrance glared at me.

I shrugged. I am Caucasian. There is no denying it.

"Shee-it," Dorrance said, stalking over to the window and glaring down at the street.

"Are they still there?" I ventured.

"Of course they still there," she said. "They'll be there until they get you. They'll be there from now until the day you lie bleeding in the street."

"Dorrance, you scaring her," Akwana said, sort of forcing a laugh to take the edge off.

"Akwana, you keep braiding her while I think of how to get her out of this."

"Okay." Akwana went in to wash the pizza off her fingers before resuming.

"Look." I faced Dorrance. "I know I don't happen to be black, but you better tell me what is going on."

She stared at me. "I don't *happen* to be black, either," she said. "My mama was black and my daddy was black and they got together on purpose to make me black."

That did make sense. But before I could apologize, she started mimicking my voice, making me sound so terribly dumb and little-girl. "I needed money," she said, taking bits of what I'd told her about the telephone return-slot ploy, "so I just yanked this plastic out and there came the money, all these quarters like it was some kind of Atlantic City slot machine." Then she spoke directly to me again. "Girl, you a fool. A flaming fool."

But by this time, Akwana, kinder and gentler and far less cryptic, was back. She listened for a second or two and then she laid a hand on my shoulder. "Robin," she said. "The money you took from the telephones belonged to those boys who are following you. It was their gig. You stole their money and they are going to get even with you for it."

"They are going to teach you a lesson," Dorrance said.

This sank in immediately. I was stealing what they had stolen. Oy. "I'll give it back," I said, my voice kind of squeaking. "Except for the six-fifty I spent on the pizza, it's right here, all of it." I was searching the room for my purse.

Akwana and Dorrance were both shaking their heads. "Too late for that," Dorrance said. "Because they gonna make an example out of you. We got to get you outta here. Akwana, you finish her up, all right?"

"All right."

While Akwana let fly her fingers yet again, I watched Dorrance moving around the shop. She pulled a set of long artificial fingernails out of a drawer and some plum-colored polish. Then she grabbed what looked like a jar of liquid makeup and held it up to consider it. She put it back, pulled out something darker. "Bittersweet chocolate," she said out loud.

"Oh-oh," Akwana said, amusement tinging the words.

"Akwana?" Dorrance asked. "Did you see those door knockers Mabel brought in the other day?"

Door knockers.

"Ha!" Akwana said. "Back scratchers and door knockers. Awright!"

"Hold it," I said. "What are door knockers? And what are back scratchers?"

Dorrance held up the fingernails. "Back scratchers," she said.

Akwana shoved a bunch of metallic things around in a drawer and produced a huge pair of squarish earrings, each earring as big as a fist. "Door knockers," she said. They reduced the earrings that Flora had worn to the status of studs.

"Honey," Dorrance told me, "when we walk outta here tonight, those boys ain't gonna bat an eye. They'll think you're just another Harlem girl out for the night."

"But first we gotta finish off your braids," Akwana said, yanking.

"You should do this under general anesthesia," I offered. It had begun to feel like dentistry on my scalp.

"You doing good," Akwana said. "Real good." Maybe by this time the Stockholm syndrome had kicked in, but I wanted her to adopt me.

Meanwhile, Dorrance applied my back scratchers. She approved of the result, regarding my hands from several different points around the room and making noises like, "Mmm-mmm-mmm," as she did so. I found them—well—extreme. Extremely extreme. But hadn't everything else about this trip been so far? Still, I felt as though my fingers were on stilts.

"One more braid," Akwana said, "and I'm done."

"Mirror, mirror," I insisted.

"One more step," she said, pulling out a Bic cigarette lighter out of her pocket and flicking it. The flame shot upward. She brought it toward me.

"Wait a minute," I said, pulling back.

"Relax," she said. "This is what holds the braids together." And she began, one by one, searing and thus sealing the end of each of the little plaits. Judging from the length of time this took, there must have been a thousand of them. The smell of singed hair erased whatever pizza odors remained.

I regressed to near infancy. "I wanna see, I wanna see," I kept whining.

"Shhh," she said.

And finally she was ready to let me do that. She wheeled my chair around toward the mirror. But she'd shrouded the mirror with a bed sheet just in case I'd been tempted to look. Now, with a flourish, she whipped the bed sheet off, and there I was. . . .

I shut my eyes, hoping that when I opened them again, the image—rather like Raggedy Ann—would disappear. But no such luck.

"My God," I said, but not because of the way I looked. Because there I was, staring at the answer. The answer. The key to what Flora had been trying to tell me about the horses' tails. It all tied in, the tails and the fashion magazines and why Flora had been killed!

If I could prove it, Jeet would be home free. And in order to prove it, I had to get to Claremont and find what I knew I was going to find, a cache of horsehair that the environmentally sensitive Mia had been using as braid with which to decorate those suits!

"Holy cow!" I said. I jumped to my feet. I started to-ward the door, and Dorrance grabbed me.

"Oh, no you don't," she said. "First you got to pay me, and second, you got to keep from getting killed by them boys in the street."

I fished Jeet's credit card out and handed it to Dorrance. She passed it on to Akwana. "Two hundred dollars," she said. I gasped and fell back into the chair. "That's exactly where I want you," she said, opening the jar of bittersweet chocolate makeup and pouring some of the mahogany liquid into the palm of her hand. "Now sit still."

"Okay, you can look now," Dorrance said.

And there I was, a Harlem girl, my skin as brown as Akwana's.

In truth, what with the door knockers and the braids, you could pretty much only see my lips, which they'd increased by pinking the middles and outlining the rim in purple. Still, Dorrance advised that I plump them fur-ther by pushing on them with my tongue. "And for God's sake," she said, "don't say a word, you hear? You say one word and those boys'll know."

"We got to give you a name," Akwana said.

"Nyoka?" I tried.

"Nyoka," Dorrance said. "That's good."

I can't remember if there was an actual character in my childhood—like in a comic book or something—named Nyoka or whether I invented her, but I recall distinctly calling myself that. Nyoka, Queen of the

Jungle, as I leaped from limb to limb in the big oak tree in our backyard. Odd, how little we change as we grow up.

"Awright, Nyoka," Dorrance said. "Here we go. Now you walk proud, you hear?"

Despite the danger, the minute we hit the pavement I began giggling. "That's good," Dorrance said. "They gonna think you're high."

High.

Except that, having solved the murder—or at least having found the motive for murder—I *was* high.

And I was especially high when my three potential assailants said things like, "Woo-we, Mama," and "Hot damn!" and "Mmmm-mmm-mmm" as Dorrance and Akwana and I, Nyoka, strutted past them, headed toward Broadway and, well, *relative* safety.

It was, by this time, eleven o'clock or so at night. I spurred myself on, imagining Jeet on his narrow prison cot. At this point, I didn't have any fear. What I had, in its place, was a lot of anger.

"This is where we split up," Akwana said. We'd come to the street where the stable was. "You be careful now, you hear?"

Dorrance seconded this. She added some pointers on hair care, however. "Get you a leave-on conditioner and spray yourself good. And the less you mess with those braids, the better. You have a problem, you just call me."

I said I would.

The three of us hugged as a unit and then they went on uptown. I headed down West Eighty-ninth toward Claremont. Even from Broadway, I could see that the bottom floor, which housed the office and manège, was all lit up, though for all I knew, they kept it that way at night. Just then, a light flared on the topmost floor as well.

I stood on the street and peered into the lighted manège. It was empty. I went around the side and used Flora's key and entered.

So far, so good.

I stood still and listened, and thought I heard the murmur of voices somewhere above me.

I made my way up the ramp to the first floor, where darkness reigned. I could tell from the sounds and the smell that horses were stabled there. This was, I remembered Flora telling me, where the box stalls started.

I listened again and determined that I'd have to go up still another flight. Meanwhile, a few of the horses nickered, as if they expected a treat. Perhaps there was a nightwatch person who came by.

If so, I was in trouble.

I tuned in for the voices again, and sure enough, there they were. I went up yet another canvas-covered ramp and discovered more horses upstairs.

Police horses.

I could tell they were police horses because by this time my eyes had adjusted to the light and I could see that this information was emblazoned on the sides of their stalls.

I racked my brain trying to remember the two newspaper articles that Flora had dumped out onto the bed at the hotel. I'd skimmed them, and remembered that they were about various people finding horses without tails.

But what else? What else?

I closed my eyes and tried self-hypnosis, and it sort of worked. Because I remembered that the articles talked about how valuable horsehair had become as a result of its rediscovery for decorative purposes.

Had there been anything about missing horses' tails at Claremont? No.

But wait a minute. There had been one—or maybe several—in New Jersey. And hadn't we arrived in New York via New Jersey? Hadn't the ride from the airport taken only about half an hour or so? So couldn't tails cut in New Jersey end up here, at Claremont?

And where was the other case that the articles had mentioned? Connecticut. Didn't all of John Cheever's people live in Connecticut and didn't they commute to New York City?

Okay, it would never have convinced a jury, but it convinced me. And it would stand to reason that Flora—a horse lover—wasn't about to let this go on. She'd probably have brought them all to justice were it not for the fact that she'd been fired and had the bad sense to mention that renowned investigative reporter, Jeet.

I inched toward the place where another ramp should have been, finding, instead, a staircase.

A filthy staircase. It seemed to be held together by the cobwebs that enveloped it.

But the sound of voices was even clearer now.

I climbed upward, waiting for the inevitable creak that would give me away. And there it was.

Creak!

* * *

I froze. The voices stopped. Then footsteps started coming my way.

Disparagement followed. "What do you think? That someone sneaked in here after us?" The voice was Sellers's.

The footsteps stopped.

Now it was answered by a voice that I remembered as belonging to Tess. "I guess you're right," she said, walking back to wherever she had been before the staircase had given me away.

"How many do we have here?" Sellers asked.

"Three hundred some," Tess answered.

Was that tails? I wondered, or hairs? Hairs wouldn't be as bad.

"Three hundred tails," Sellers said. "That's quite a haul."

My stomach flipped over.

Of course horses can live without tails, but they use them a lot. They communicate with them, in addition to using them to swish flies. And they're amazingly articulate. I had a gelding who would indignantly smack me across the face with his tail whenever I tried to clean his sheath.

Three hundred tails! Three hundred horses bereft!

I should back out, I thought. Leave and get myself to the nearest police station. But that would mean passing over the step that had betrayed my presence once. Next time I might not be as lucky.

But also, I couldn't imagine the New York City police, busy as they were with all the other crimes, paying a few missing horses' tails any mind. How could they possibly? What was more, I just knew I'd have the devil of a time convincing them that horse tails had somehow added up to murder.

.No.

I had to stay and see this through.

It was up to me.

In the back of my head, I could hear Jeet's voice. "Horses," he'd be saying, "that's how both of us got into this. Horses."

And it was true. If I'd never gone to Flora's, if I'd never gone to Claremont, Jeet would be sitting across from me at some fabulous New York restaurant and we'd be arguing about whether something with a French name had too much paprika in it or not.

Instead, I was trapped in a cobwebbed stairwell with probably every spider in America lying in wait. Or—I heard a slight rustling sound—worse.

Worse.

Because there, on the step that was even with my eyes, was a mouse.

A cute mouse, gray, with pink-tipped ears and paws. As long as it stood still, I was okay.

If it started running, it would be like gasping on the plane whenever the pilot turned: I'd react in sheer reflex.

If it started running, I would not be able to keep my cool.

Think about Jeet, I counseled myself, even as beads of sweat were forming on my brow. Steady. Steady. Jeet's freedom depends on you!

Then the mouse took off and I shot up the staircase

as if fired from a cannon, my loud, shrill scream pene-
trating the night air.

When I reached the landing that marked the third
floor, I found Tess and Sellers flattened against one of
the sooty walls. Tess was quaking.

Long strands of horsehair—tails, I assume—were everywhere.

"You people are criminals!" I said. For emphasis, I
stuck my hands on my hips. I think I was quaking, too,
what with the mouse and now seeing this.

They both looked at me. Then they smiled and
looked at each other. It had dawned on both of them
that I was sans weapon, no way at all of dealing with
them. Unless you count my anger.

And they didn't.

Sellers came toward me. "And just what do you plan
to do about it?"

Sellers looked even more menacing than usual, his
left eye developing some sort of nervous tic as he no
doubt pondered rending me limb from limb.

"You keep away from me," I said, backing up and
tripping over something and falling.

From my vantage point on the ground, I saw what
had made me fall: an enormous gray cat.

The cat took advantage of my plight and rubbed up
against me, purring.

"It's Mouse," Tess said. "Good boy, Mouse."

At the word *mouse*, I lifted my legs and tried to lev-
erage myself upright, but Sellers pushed my shoulder
and thwarted that attempt in the bud.

"Stay down," he growled, "while we decide what we're going to do to you."

I lay there. The cat came and sat just below my chin. He purred and kneaded his claws on my chest. Every now and then one would penetrate my clothing and I'd gasp.

Whenever I gasped, Tess and Sellers would stop whatever they were murmuring about and listen for a minute. Then they'd resume.

I thought they were arguing about how to do me in. Since Claremont was a relatively low structure, they couldn't rely on their old standby of pushing me out the window. I mean, I could survive.

I sat up, catching hold of Mouse and moving him to my lap. That was okay with him. He settled there as if he hadn't even been moved.

I watched Tess and Sellers. Every now and then they looked over at me, but mostly they were busy with each other and their debate.

I stood up. I was still holding Mouse, cradling him the way you would a baby.

They glanced at me, but didn't seem to think it was important.

I was about twenty feet away. I began walking toward them. I knew what I was going to do. I was going to, when I got close enough, toss Mouse at them and run. Because Mouse could handle it, he would be all right. And my action would be so unbelievably fast and unpredictable that it would take Tess and Sellers a while to recover, and by that time I'd be out of here.

* * *

Maybe cats are as intuitive as people say. Because Mouse all of a sudden didn't want me holding him. He began to writhe and make pretty ghastly noises.

"Put him down," Sellers said, walking toward me.

That was when I launched the cat, aiming for Sellers's face.

I heard a yowl that could have been either of them, Mouse or Sellers. And I was scooting down the cobwebbed stairwell toward, I hoped, freedom, or help at least.

"I'll kill you for that," I heard Sellers say behind me.

Then his meaty hand closed over several of my braids and began to pull.

I told you that Akwana and Dorrance had extended my hair, made it thicker and longer by adding artificial hair the color of my own. So what Sellers got—and I really would have given anything to see his face—was, quite literally, a handful of braids. Because the artificial part he'd grabbed on to came off in his hand.

This time the pain I felt as the artificial hair separated from my own real hair was worth it.

I even laughed a little as I continued racing down, now, to three.

Behind me now I heard Tess shouting, "Move! Get her, get her!" and then some scuffling, as if Tess and Sellers were disagreeing physically on what steps to take. Then Tess said, "Get out of my way, you moron."

Sellers, evidently, had been so stunned by getting my hair in his hand that he'd actually frozen, blocking Tess's way.

What a break! I weighed whether to keep running or to hide, and opted for the latter. Then later on, when they'd given up their search, I'd get away.

Meanwhile, the horses, sensing that something was awry, were whinnying and running in little circles in their stalls. Only one of them seemed calm and that was a police horse, who looked over at me as if memorizing my description so that he could pick me up out of a lineup.

I slid the bolt on his stall and crept in beside him.

And just in time. Sellers and Tess were hot on my trail. The building shook as Sellers trundled down the stairs, Tess in his wake. Then they stood mere feet away from the spot where I'd hidden.

They were arguing.

"What difference does it make?" Sellers was saying. "No matter what she does, it won't make a bit of difference because the truck will be here in a minute. And once they take the tails away, who's gonna believe her? A tourist, for God's sake. A tourist in blackface."

Oh. I'd forgotten about that. I tried to rub my face with my big top, but that made my door knockers jangle.

"Did you hear that?" Tess said.

"No. What was it?"

"It was like, I don't know, bells."

"Tess, you're losing it. Come on. Let's get those tails ready and get out of here."

"You're right," Tess said. "But if Mia finds out about her . . ."

'What?" Sellers asked. "She'll make you do away with her the way you did with Flora?"

"You're crazy," Tess said. "I didn't do away with anyone. It was Mia herself. She heard what happened and was so damned flustered that she came here in the limo and then lit off like there was no tomorrow."

I remembered the black-garbed figure I'd seen coming into the stable. But the person who had followed me hadn't been in a car. That person had been on foot. And hadn't Sellers, when we were in the coffee place, said *he'd* followed me? What were we? A veritable procession, moving through the streets of Manhattan, everyone in creation behind me as I'd made my way to the hotel? And even if that was true, it still didn't explain, for sure, which person in that procession had actually gone up to the room and killed poor Flora.

Detective work can be the pits.

Outside someone honked.

"The truck," Tess said.

I had a reprieve.

It probably took about an hour to load the tails into the truck. Crouched over as I was, it felt like five. I could have yielded to the temptation to sprawl, but there wasn't anything to guarantee that the police horse who was sharing his stall with me wouldn't spook. And now I was trapped in the stall while Tess and Sellers and several others trooped from the street level to the top floor and back again.

"Come on, come on, come on," someone whose

voice was unfamiliar urged. "You know how traffic gets."

It seemed lighter outside. Predawn nautical twilight, I believe it's technically called.

"Come *on*." That voice again.

"What's your problem? We get faster every time," Sellers said.

"I think this is your last shipment," the voice told him.

"What do you mean?" Tess asked.

"Boss lady's leaving the country. It was in all the gossip columns. She's moving her operations to Brazil or someplace."

Sellers had been walking around as he spoke. Now he was right beside my horse's door. "Is that so?" he said.

"Yeah. An hour, hour and a half from now, she'll be on her way."

Brazil. The land of no extradition. Where Mia could, quite literally, get away from it all.

I shut my eyes and saw Flora. What would Flora have done? She'd have nailed Mia, that was what. She'd have captured her, made her pay.

But where was Mia? How could I get to her?

"Could you speed it up, please?" the voice said. "I'm telling you, traffic on Seventh Avenue is a bitch."

Seventh Avenue.

Finally they all went downstairs, freeing me, more or less. Well, actually, less, since I could still hear them chatting away on a lower level. But it was enough of a respite to let me decide what it was I was going to do.

I was going to tack up this police horse and escape the building on him.

Then I'd ride him over to Seventh Avenue, wherever that was, and capture the illustrious and elusive designer, Mia. Mia, who had pushed poor Flora to her death.

Except that—well, come on, you know there's always something that'll go wrong—the next thing I heard was Tess, her voice unusually melodious as she said, "I'll have him ready in a jiff."

And the next thing I knew, she was coming toward my stall. In a minute she'd be whipping open the stall door. God!

There isn't much room to hide in a box stall. So I went underground. Burrowed, that is, under a wad of hay and the wood shavings and—yes—whatever droppings the police horse had made.

Sure enough, the stall door opened.

"Well, I'll be," Tess said.

But it wasn't because she'd seen me. I was sufficiently buried.

No. She'd said it because she had come to tack the park policeman's horse up for him and lo! There he was, ready to go. Because I'd just done it.

She evidently thought Sellers had, because she shouted, "Thanks, Sellers," almost deafening both the horse and me, before clucking the horse out. "Come on, Finny," she said. "Come on."

I had never seen anyone cluck to get a horse to come to them. Usually, if you cluck at all, you cluck to make the horse go faster or get more enthusiastic about what he's doing—say, approaching a jump or something.

But there she was, *cluck cluck cluck.* I could imagine Finny just standing there, staring at her. Finally she walked off, leaving the stall door open.

I stood up and began brushing myself off. I don't know if you know what shavings are like, but they're smaller than chips. They're these little flakes of wood, and so they are especially clingy.

A good number of them, to be sure, were clinging to me. I continued to swipe at myself.

The next thing I heard was her voice coming over the loudspeaker. "Finny. Finny."

And Finny went into automaton mode and trooped out.

I abandoned my self-grooming efforts and went right behind him.

Should I mount? I wondered. Then I realized that the doorways were way too low. I'd be decapitated if I did. So I kept right on behind.

From floor two to one.

Where a U.S. Park Policeman—if that's what they're called—stood in full regalia, awaiting his steed.

I paused briefly—was I wanted for anything? It seemed to me I was in the clear, except for stealing the coins from the telephone, which of course the officer couldn't have known about. So I could walk tall.

Except that Tess spotted me.

"My God," she said. "There she is!"

Sellers poked his head out of the office, regarding

me. The officer did, too. "Get her!" Tess yelled. "Get her! She broke in here last night. We've been looking for her."

The Park Policeman stepped toward me, a furrow between his brows.

Fin stood dutifully at the mounting block.

I looked at Fin. I could vault onto him and take off just like that. I could capture Mia exactly as I'd planned. I could—

"Officer," I yelled at the Policeman, "these people are criminals. You have to arrest them."

The Policeman looked exceedingly puzzled, and Sellers and Tess started yelling at him that each of them was working undercover and that he should be assisting them in the apprehension of—

"Where is Seventh Avenue?" I called, interrupting, stepping onto the mounting block and dropping a leg over Fin in a single motion.

Sellers pointed one way and Tess another.

"Which way?" I screamed, looking at the officer.

He opened his mouth, but shut it again when Sellers and Tess repeated what they'd said.

"Believe me," Sellers urged. "I'm an undercover investigator. Animal rights. I wouldn't lie to you."

"*I'm* an undercover investigator," Tess said. "*I'm* telling the truth."

"Flora was screwing up my investigation," Sellers said. "I wanted her gone, yes, but gone from Claremont. Gone so I could nail these bastards." He sighed. "Listen," he said, pointing in the direction of Central Park. "Turn right at the park and then go all the way to the end. Then cut over to Broadway and keep going."

"Turn *left* at the park," Tess shouted. "Turn *left*."

"Get off that horse," the Park Policeman said. "This instant, do you hear?"

"Left," Tess said.

"No, right," Sellers argued.

I looked at both of them. Flora had hated Sellers, it was true, but then again, maybe he was good at undercover work, so good that he seemed bad. She hadn't said a word about Tess. Still, Tess was the one who clucked when she wanted Fin to come to her, whereas I had seen Sellers ride and could tell that he knew what he was doing. And one of the first things Sellers had asked me was whether or not Lars had made his way back to the stable okay.

So, no question: I believed Sellers.

I closed my legs on Finny and took off toward Central Park, bent on turning right.

CHAPTER 9

I galloped down the narrow pavement that fronted a row of brownstones, my mind going every bit as fast as Finny's hooves. Flora had found the tails, the long streaming tails that I'd seen Sellers and Tess stacking and counting on the uppermost floor. So of course the *Claremont* horses weren't tailless when I'd gone to reconnoiter. Flora had found the tails that had belonged to countless horses in New Jersey and Connecticut and probably upstate New York as well. Someone—Tess, I'd assume—had been using Claremont as a base for some very base operations. And Sellers *was* an undercover investigator who had been working to expose whoever it was.

Poor Flora. She'd somehow stumbled onto the Mia connection. Perhaps on one of the sleepless nights that she described, the nights when she'd let herself into the stable to groove on the contentment in the atmosphere.

Sure. I could see it. Flora huddled in the darkness hearing Tess come in. And then the limo drives up with Mia herself in it. Flora, on her own, had been making a case against Mia, all right. That was the point of all those fashion magazines. I got tears in my eyes thinking about the magnitude of bravery that a thing like that took.

But beyond all that, was what Mia was doing actually against the law?

How had Flora known where the horsehair was coming from? Had she maybe followed the culprits on one of their forays into the New York suburbs? Had she accompanied them, pretending to be among their number? Would I ever know?

I looked behind me, but all I could see was what looked at first like snow. Then I realized what it was: the shavings that had adhered to me were being sucked off by the wake that I was creating.

Meanwhile, Fin was approaching the low stone wall that enclosed the park. In the dim near-morning light, I looked for a spot where I wouldn't get slammed into a branch.

I was, I knew, going to jump.

I used to love jumping, would jump every chance I got. Now, when I think of some of the things I've jumped, I blanch. I jumped them when I thought I was invincible.

Once, in a clinic, my horse stepped on the pole that was supposed to serve as a takeoff point for a very small fence. The horse went down to one knee. And collectively, the audience—because this was a heavily attended clinic with a woman who had been on our Olympic three-day team—sucked in its breath.

But even from this ungainly stance, my horse pushed off those hind legs and made it over the jump without incident. A minor miracle, if you will.

The clinician knew it. "This horse will never fall," she pronounced, and because I believed it, I rode like blazes. Invincible, as I said.

Then one day it happened. I don't even know for sure what. All I know is that the horse hooked a front leg on something that didn't budge and the next thing I knew we were both upside down and then right side up and then upside down again.

I remember the sequence as I saw it all too vividly: mane and sky and mane and sky and mane.

The next thing I knew, I was being told not to move, not that I could. Off in the distance, I could hear a siren coming closer and then stopping at what seemed an enormously far-off place.

Then someone put a cervical collar around my neck and people one-two-three-lifted me onto a stretcher.

Someone said, as I was carried through the woods to the place where the ambulance had had to stop, that my horse was fine, and it was only then I realized that I'd fallen with her. Only then that I remembered.

But then once I had, I couldn't forget. I'd walk toward a log six inches in diameter on the ground, and I'd remember, mane and sky and mane and sky and freeze.

I never wanted, after that, to ever jump again.

Except that now, here I was, on a horse I'd never ridden before, aiming at a solid stone wall with God only knew on the other side.

And here we go . . .

. . . landing about three feet lower on the far side than on the side we'd taken off—the equivalent, I'd say, of an advanced jump, or prelim at least.

But there wasn't any time to congratulate myself or Finny, who seemed to love all this. Because Central Park is not a flat, well-manicured expanse by any means.

Oh, no. Central Park is, well, made to look natural, or left to. Which means that there are hills and dales and boulders and gorges.

At the same time, there are dogs roaming (illegally) off leash while their owners yell at them to watch out for the horse.

And there are man-made obstacles, like steps.

Yes, steps. Steps that loomed before I even had a chance to be afraid.

Finny took them as one would a spread. God, I pity the felon who took off with Finny in pursuit.

But then—I guess we were maybe three blocks into the park—we came upon what seemed an impassible sector, more steps, only ultrasteep and more than any horse could leap in a single bound. "Oh, Jeez," I said, and Finny began to veer left.

What was happening?

Well, what was happening was that Finny, who had been ridden in this park Lord only knew how many times a week, was going the way that he knew. And now I saw what that was. He was heading toward a bridge that would enable us to bypass the staircase.

Awright, Finny!

Where had the Parks Department gotten this horse? Was he a retired eventer? Why had he been retired? Was he for sale? He didn't seem to hesitate at anything, not even the Marionette Theater (which was so labeled) that loomed on our left, nor at the heavy road equipment that was stored on our right.

Plum or Spier, of course, would still have been trying to get up the nerve to cross Amsterdam. But then, how many horses could be expected to have Finny's city smarts?

So on past the bulldozers and front-end loaders. On and on and on.

What would I do? I thought. Would I tie Finny to a hydrant and run up into Mia's studio and grab her by her horsehair-braided lapels? And how would I find Mia's studio? Oy.

Then I became aware of a police car just beyond the park wall on what would be Central Park West. A police car with what looked like Sellers hanging out of the driver's seat and hollering something.

I couldn't risk stopping to ask what. After all, I'd commandeered a Park Policeman's horse. That was probably a felony. Only if I managed to capture Mia could I hope to redeem myself, right?

Then, beyond the cop car, I saw it in all its Gothic splendor: the Dakota, it had to be. The Dakota, where John Lennon had lived—and died. The Dakota, where *Rosemary's Baby* had been filmed. God, the actual Dakota.

Which is how I ended up headed right into an arbor of some kind. Not that it bothered Finny one bit. I had been looking off to my right, and when I faced forward again, there it was. Otherwise I could have gone around it.

Finny's hooves hit the hollow wooden bridge that was the base of the arbor. And you'd think that would have alerted the little Filipino man who was setting up a T-shirt display at the other end, wouldn't you?

But it didn't. We didn't hit him, but we did graze the counter he'd been erecting sufficiently to scatter several dozen T-shirts hither and yon.

He cursed at us, I think.

And we rode on.

I don't know how far we'd gone, but Finny was handling it easily. I wondered, in fact, if the Policeman hadn't galloped him each and every day. It was no accident that the horse was so fit.

Then there was what, for Finny, proved to be a major distraction.

The Tavern on the Green.

Not the Tavern on the Green per se, but the horse-drawn carriages parked in front of it alongside several stretch limos.

I told you about herd instinct. It governs much of what horses do. We have to overcome it in order to ride them. Finny succumbed to it.

And stopped dead.

Nothing in Finny's behavior hitherto had led me to expect such a thing, and so I was wholly unprepared. I was carried forward by my own momentum, and sailed over the horse's neck and head and landed, *whump!* on the pavement. *Whump!* Right in front of—and I'm not kidding—a life-size topiary rendition of King Kong, his mighty green fist upraised.

Only in New York.

And Finny was no gentleman. He turned tail and raced over to schmooze with the carriage horses, trotting round to visit with a large dapple gray, then a

finely chiseled bay, and then halting at the side of a
chestnut with a flaxen mane and tail.

The chestnut's driver—a young woman in a top hat—
began shouting at me. "You can't run a horse like that
and just let it stand," she said. "You have to cool it out.
Walk it."

"I know, I know," I said, dusting myself off. "But
I'm not finished yet. I have to go all the way to Seventh
Avenue."

As I spoke I gathered up Finny's reins and positioned
my stirrup so that I could mount.

"Why?" the young woman asked.

"It's too long a story. But I have to get this designer,
Mia."

"Mia? She was just here."

"What?"

"Just left. In that white limo." She pointed at a pair
of tail fins disappearing even as we spoke.

"What? Did she just have breakfast?"

"They're doing a fashion shoot here. We're in on it.
That's why we're all here, you know, the horses and
stuff."

"Oh, yeah," I said. "Well, tell the other drivers to
come over here, because I've got some stuff you all
ought to hear about Mia. In fact, you can help me nail
her."

We went around the fountain at Columbus Circle and
then, in procession, made our way down Broadway,
where all the traffic flowed in our direction now.

We passed the theaters I'd longed to see when first I

came. Passed the marquees announcing *Cats* and *Miss Saigon.*

We passed the place where David Letterman films his show. Passed an ad for *Tommy* and a Peter Townshend art show.

We passed with determination, horse lovers on a mission. The owner of the chestnut knew exactly where Mia's studio was and told me the address of the building lest we get separated.

And on the way we passed the truck that held all the horsehair, gridlocked in an incredible traffic jam. The police car that Sellers was driving had stopped as close to it as it could get, which was still pretty far away. The two who had manned the truck were being loaded into what I assume is still called a paddy wagon.

In the back of the car that Sellers occupied was Tess.

And in the front seat was the Park Policeman. The Policeman leaned out as I neared on Finny. "How's he doing?" he asked.

I didn't tell him about Finny's rude stop. "He's great," I said, which was basically, even with the stop, quite true.

"Yeah, I love the old boy," the Policeman said.

God, what is it that horses have? When you love them, you love them. You love them all. Not just the well-trained, finely bred ones, but all of them. The kickers and the buckers and the cribbers and the badasses, too. You just do. There should be a support group for people hooked on horses. "He's quite a guy," I said.

"Mia's studio coming up," the young woman with the chestnut called back to us. The carriage seemed narrow enough to go where cars could not. "Wait a minute," Sellers called, and he opened the door and stood as the handcuffed Tess climbed out. Sellers reached back in and pulled out a bulky black vinyl case.

"We'll go along," he said, lifting Tess into the first carriage. "I think Tessie here ought to see this."

The Park Policeman climbed into one of the other carriages and waved. Finny and I got behind the rig pulled by the chestnut.

"What do we do now?" the driver asked when we arrived at the address that was Mia's.

"We wait," Sellers said.

New York reporters have a nose for news. Or else, from the sky, a group of horse-drawn vehicles meandering through the garment district seems newsworthy. Because we hadn't been there five minutes when a news helicopter started buzzing us.

The horses, as usual, were unperturbed. What would it take, I wondered, to rattle a New York City horse?

Sellers walked over to Finny and me, black case in hand. He unzipped it and handed me a small, battery-powered video camera. "Listen," he hollered over the sound of the rotors above us, "I have a friend in the Bureau of Immigration and Naturalization. She thinks there might be more at stake here than animal rights. So, do me a favor, okay?" He gestured at a row of casement windows down a narrow walkway. A row that you couldn't see into without a ladder—or a horse.

I took the camera, leaned down so that he could click the right buttons to power it, and moved Fin in that direction.

Sellers and his Immigration friend were right. There in the viewfinder was a classic sweatshop scene. Women and children jammed together at long tables braiding piles and piles of horsehair, and Mia stalking the aisleways policing their efforts.

I looked over at Sellers and yelled, "You're right!" Which was totally the wrong move.

When I looked back, everyone in the room, Mia included, was staring at me. Or at the camera, at least.

Mia made a face that looked like that Munch painting *The Scream*, and bolted toward an exit sign.

I glanced down the walkway and saw a metal door. I trotted down past the door so that I could turn her if she emerged. Turn her and send her back to Sellers and company at the other end.

Sure enough, she came clattering out, looking both ways and opting for the one that I had hoped to block. I had the video camera under my arm, which meant I had to hold the reins with just one hand. Finny seemed eager beneath me, as though he'd figured the whole thing out.

But I saw something he didn't. Mia holding a long, daggerlike sewing needle in her hand.

"Get out of my way"—she sneered—"or I'll sink this so fast your horse won't know what hit it." Her voice was like a cleaver. Her face was contorted to match it. Finny, beneath me, quivered, understanding the threat all too well. Oh, he didn't understand the words, but he understood the tone, the posture.

"You would hurt this horse?" I said, incredulity ting-

ing my voice. All that stuff in the article I'd read about
how she cared about animals!

"This horse means as much to me as a pound of
lunch meat," she said.

I longed for a microphone, dangling from the helicopter overhead, to catch her awful statement, but even
if there had been one, the deafening noise from the rotors would have drowned Mia out. Perhaps the news
station employed a lip-reader?

Then I realized that a lip-reader wouldn't be necessary. The camera under my arm was still turned on. I
would be getting video of maybe my armpit, but the
audio—that would be intact.

Finny was antsy underneath me and I realized that,
hey, he wasn't afraid. He was eager. He was getting
ready to play "Nail the Perp."

I looked at the needle. Unless Mia was possessed of
some arcane veterinary knowledge, I reasoned, how
much could this needle hurt the horse? I mean, how different could it be from a tetanus shot, which horses
don't even appear to notice getting?

"Go, Finny." I pressed him forward, right at her, and
he didn't even hesitate. He was a police horse through
and through. No kidding, you could have ridden him
smack into cannon fire.

I guess Mia wasn't expecting that. She jumped back
reflexively, turned, and ran toward certain capture.
Without any cue from me, Finny went after her.

But wouldn't you know? At the end of the alleyway,
Sellers and the crew had moved down toward the entrance to the building, and Mia was able to duck onto
the street and head the other way.

"Hey!" I called out, hoping someone heard me.

Even though Finny had more speed, Mia had the advantage here, where the street had come alive with men pulling racks of clothing, unloading cartons, and carrying mannequins and such. I had to, much to Finny's chagrin, walk him through this morass even as Mia was running.

Still, I could see the carriages farther on up the street, and I knew that, no matter what, Mia wasn't going to get away from us.

We horse lovers are a determined lot.

What tripped her up, though, was pretty much the same thing that had made me nearly miss the arbor. She was busy looking at something else. The something else was a rustic display—a bed of hay upon which had been erected a cedar fence, a waterfall, and some cactus—all of this in front of a store announcing that it sold theatrical props.

Mia was looking at it and tripped. The long silver needle bounced out of her hand and landed—yes!—in the haystack.

But she was no quitter.

She was on her feet and hoofing it before Finny and I could get to her.

Except how far could she go? Surely she could see the wagons up ahead as well as we could.

But it didn't come to that. We managed to overtake her at a street post, and we crowded in, pressing her tiny little body up against it as hard as we dared. Mia wheeled, and so did Finny, intent on his prey.

"Was that a canter pirouette?" the Park Policeman, who'd come running up, wanted to know.

If so, it was my first, and one-handed, too! I smiled enigmatically and handed the camera to him.

And overhead, the helicopter swooped down and hovered.

I thought about that lunch-meat statement and the way she'd brandished that long silver needle. I yelled at the copter—fruitlessly, I'll bet. "Check her apartment. I'll give you ten to one all her shoes and purses aren't vinyl."

Sellers came lumbering up. "Great work," he said. "We've got enough." Enough to reveal to the world what a hypocrite this Mia was. Enough to expose her abuse of humans. And her own cruel form of horse abuse.

The Park Policeman took Finny from me so that I could accompany Sellers and Mia and Tess to the precinct house. It was like old home week there. It turned out that the blacksmith, Flora's old beau, knew that Mia had followed me, yes, but only after she'd learned that Tess had taken my address and gone to my hotel. Sellers had been third in line, and way too late to make a difference. It *had* been a procession at that.

It wasn't Mia who murdered Flora; it was Tess. Sellers said that maybe Jeet would be able to pick Tess out of a lineup. Jeet had caught a glimpse of her, you'll remember, when he came into the room while Flora and Tess were struggling. But it didn't much matter, because Tess, once booked, had confessed.

It turned out, further, that the man on the balcony—the one with the marigolds—*was* a spy after all. He was a spy for the same animal-rights organization that Sellers worked for, and he had photos of Mia emerging from the limo and entering Claremont.

I felt sort of bad that Tubular and Akwana and Dorrance weren't there at the end as well. It would have been super if everyone had turned out to be an undercover something or other, except that life isn't like that, alas.

In life people like Flora—beautiful, talented people—get killed, and for stupid pointless reasons.

And speaking of those reasons, the police now had the truck with the horses' tails themselves. Considering the way Mia's need for horsehair had driven up the cost of it, the charge, someone said, could be grand larceny.

All that remained to worry about, it seemed, was Jeet.

"Uh, excuse me," I said to Sellers, "but my husband was arrested and—"

"Oh, right." He reached for the phone.

CHAPTER 10

I had expected to find out how I could visit Jeet or arrange bail or something like that. What I learned, however, was that Jeet had been released shortly after questioning. And where was he? He'd evidently given the police the address of the hotel where we had been staying—the very hotel that had unceremoniously evicted me.

But surely Jeet wouldn't be in *that* room, would he?

I called and asked for the room, and a surly someone who was not my husband answered.

Well, that was a relief.

But first things first.

I went to the first hair salon I came to that was open and asked them to undo my braids.

"That'll cost you," the hairdresser said. "It'll take about seven hours to undo those."

"Seven hours."

"Plus it's a shame. Whoever did them did a beautiful job! Just a beautiful job."

"I know, but—"

"The customer is always right," he finished.

"But is there anything that could speed things up?" I asked. "And keep the cost down?"

"Well ..." He stood back and pursed his lips. "You could whack them, I suppose."

"Whack them?"

"You know, cut them off. That wouldn't take any time at all. Of course, it would leave you with short hair."

"Whack away," I said, although last year at this time I had promised myself I would let my hair grow. Oh, well.

The result was a pixielike me.

And best of all, the shop had a shower and the proprietor let me use it, so I was no longer swathed in bittersweet chocolate makeup. They were able to get my back scratcher nails off, too. Amazing how they'd held up through all of this!

Now on to the hotel, where I confronted an unctuous and therefore exceedingly apologetic manager named Winesap. He tried to sugar me out of my anger, but I held firm.

"You evicted me," I said, "as though I were some sort of . . . trollop."

Winesap quivered at the word. Then he drew himself up full height. "The man who evicted you has been fired," he soothed. "And if it's any consolation, the hotel will not be charging you and your husband for your stay. In fact, the hotel will even provide the meals you've eaten and the calls you've made on a complimentary basis."

There was please-don't-sue written all over him.

"Hmmm," I said.

"Will that be agreeable?" he asked.

"I'm not sure," I said.

"Look, we're comping you," he said, the starch in his delivery replaced by a healthier Brooklynese. "So what do you want already?"

"Okay, okay," I said.

Then I got the room number and a key and a message that had been left for me and went upstairs.

I read the message in the elevator. It was from Wanda and had been phoned in. It said: *Beware the Gorilla.*

It was a good thing I hadn't gotten it earlier, because I'd have thought that Sellers was the gorilla when in fact he was one of the good guys.

Then I thought of the other part that Wanda had earlier divined, about something falling from the sky.

Poor Flora. Even though I hadn't known her long, I doubted that I'd ever forget her. I ached whenever the thought of her came into my mind.

When I opened the door to our room, I found Jeet curled on the bed in fetal position, asleep. His hair was tousled and he was breathing deeply, contentedly. I looked over at our travel clock. It was 9:30 A.M. Just about twenty-four hours since he and I had sat across the breakfast table from each other downstairs.

As if he knew I was in the room, he stretched and smiled in his sleep. I went over and sat down. I stroked his shoulder and his eyes fluttered open. "G'morning," he said. "What time did you get in?"

"Late," I said.

"Where were you?"

"I was, uh, getting my hair done." Well, hadn't I been?

He squinted up at me, focusing. "Oh," he said. "Looks cute."

"Thanks."

He shut his eyes and started drifting back to sleep.

I couldn't stand waiting to hear. I nudged him. "So what was it like, being arrested?"

He sat up. "They were very nice about the whole thing," he said. "It was just a misunderstanding."

"Browning at the paper never called," I tattled.

"Yes, he did. He called one of the DAs and straightened everything out. They went to college together or something."

"Oh."

"Poor Robin," he said. "You must be bored stiff."

"No."

"You're just saying that."

"No." Then I remembered why we were here. "What about your book thing, though?"

"It's a done deal," he told me. "Maggie picked me up at police headquarters and we met with the publisher at Le Cirque and . . . you're looking at a man with a book contract."

"Oh, Jeet," I said, leaning into him.

"As a matter of fact, do you know which sample chapter he liked best?"

"Which one?"

"The one about how we met," Jeet said.

I told you Jeet was going to write a food memoir. Well, the fact is, Jeet approached me at a college party because of food.

I was, of course, on a diet. So all I had eaten that day was a big fat juicy ripe tomato.

Except that I sort of doctored it up with some basil, olive oil, salt, pepper, and—well, okay—a head of garlic.

No, I didn't mean to say a clove, I meant the head, with however many cloves there were in it.

Let me put it this way: if there were vampires around, they weren't about to approach me. I was safe.

But no one else seemed to want to approach me either.

Except for Jeet, who tracked me like a bloodhound.

My first view of him, in fact, was with his nostrils twitching. "What did you have for dinner?" he asked.

And I said, "Dinner?"

And won his heart.

"Here, look," he said, handing me a recipe he'd handwritten:

Meet Your Mate Tomatoes

Slice super-ripe tomatoes as thinly as you can without savaging them. Slice fresh garlic—less than a head, if you're a coward—likewise and toss atop tomatoes. Sprinkle on basil, less if dried, though fresh is better. Brandish salt and pepper, then drizzle with olive oil. Serve with hot French bread for mopping.

"Oh, Jeet," I said. "This is so sweet."

"Let's go out and have breakfast," he said. "I'll see what the weather is." He flipped the television on and one of those morning blond women appeared. "I'll get ready," he said. "You pay attention and call me when the local news comes on."

"It's on," I said, and then almost instantly regretted calling him. Because there, on the screen, was a shot of me riding Finny through the streets, hot on Mia's trail.

"Jeet, I—" I began, but he was rapt.

"Look at this, Robin," he said. "A horse!" He turned the sound up.

"Oh, wait, we don't need to turn it up so loud," I said, moving forward. "I mean, people might be sleeping."

Jeet looked at me strangely and then put his arm around me. "No, come on," he said. "You don't want to miss this." And with his other hand he reached forward and turned the sound up even more.

". . . captured by an unidentified black woman," the announcer was saying. Then they played Mia's voice, the thing she'd said about the horse mattering as much as a pound of lunch meat.

So now the world did know.

"What a terrible woman," Jeet said.

"Who would have thought?" I added, and sighed. I steeled myself for the inevitable moment when Jeet would connect me with the woman in the saddle. In fact, I was almost ready to confess when the gods smiled down at me and ended the news bite by mercifully freezing the frame.

But when the frame froze, I saw something I hadn't seen while the whole thing had been happening. God, it was a perfect end, too:

I'd pinned Mia just below a street sign reading FASH-ION, which, evidently, is another name for Seventh Avenue. And below that, one of the animal-rights people had hung yet another sign, a sign Mia should have heeded.

It said: COMPASSION.

"Amen," Jeet said, giving my shoulder a squeeze.

Carolyn Banks

Published by Fawcett Books.
Available in your local bookstore.